A Fake Courtship

HISTORICAL REGENCY ROMANCE

Sally Forbes

Table of Contents

Prologue

Anne Huxley nervously clutched a flute of champagne, nursing it gently to make it last as long as possible to prevent the need to fetch another and risk drawing attention to herself. The grand ballroom of her family's estate was alive with cheery music, graceful dancers, and animated conversations all around her. The crystal chandeliers cast a warm glow over the glossy wood floor, making the purple line patterns arranged on the dance floor in such a way as to help guide the dancers shimmer like thin, regal pools.

The pale lavender walls of the ballroom added to the sense of royalty to the room, and the pink swags that curved between the pillars that separated the musician's gallery and the refreshment setup on opposite sides of the room from the dance floor and mingling circle just outside the dancing area. Both areas were lit by their own smaller chandeliers, showcasing the crisp black and white suits of the orchestra members and the champagne flutes, wine glasses and array of cheeses, bread, fruit and cakes, respectively.

The orchestra's latest cotillion filled the air and several couples displayed perfect grace as they performed the dance. Laughter blended seamlessly with the music, creating a cheerful, lighthearted atmosphere. Yet, amidst the splendor and grandeur of the party, Anne Huxley felt anything but at ease. She noticed with chagrin that her glass was nearly empty, and she would have to weave her way through clusters of party guests to get another. And in her bright yellow gown that her mother, the viscountess of Huxley, had insisted she wear, she was sure to draw eyes right to her. Especially the eyes of her distant cousin, who had been relentlessly pursuing her all evening.

Her jade green eyes darted around the room, searching for Albert Harrow. Her distant cousin was a man whose ambition far outweighed his charm. On that evening, he was also fueled by the spirits being served at the party, which made him even bolder in his advances toward her. The hungry gleam in his eyes was impossible to miss, and his endless chasing and sloppy attempts at trapping her in conversation all evening had left Anne on edge.

Shuddering at the idea of having to dance with her distasteful cousin, Anne decided she would take a chance on slipping over to the refreshment tables. She ducked into the crowd as though she was heading for the entryway to the ballroom, intending to slip around the crowd and sneak up to the tables from behind them. There, she could hide behind one of the pillars and maintain a vantage point that would allow her to keep an eye out for the insufferable man.

She was just about to round the first pillar that stood between the refreshment tables and the dance floor, just paces from the outermost dancers, when a figure bumped into her. She had her eyes on the ground, but she recognized the deep purple breeches and matching boots immediately.

"Pardon me, Albert," she mumbled, hoping he was at last too inebriated to stop her from getting away.

She was terribly mistaken. He reached out and took her hand, a gentlemanly gesture in itself, but his grip spoke of his determination to not release her.

"Anne, my beloved," he drawled, the alcohol on his breath seeping into the air and nearly choking Anne. "Where have you been hiding? I've been looking for you."

Anne lifted her gaze, carefully avoiding her cousin's, pretending to be searching for someone.

"I need to speak to Mother," she said quickly, attempting to sound as though it was an urgent matter.

Albert pretended as though she hadn't spoken. He raised her hand to his lips, planting a kiss across her knuckles. Even with her gloves, she could feel the drool he left in the wake of his sloppy kiss, and her stomach churned.

"I must insist that you dance with me before the evening ends," he said. "In fact, I would have no complaints if you should decide to dance the final waltz with me."

Anne's stomach flipped again, and she feared that her champagne would end up all over the front of her cousin's coat. Being fifteen years her senior, his hair was graying at the temples and in streaks all over what remained of his black hair. But that wasn't what repulsed her. He was looking at her like a lion might look at a gazelle before pouncing to gain its meal. She shook her head, trying to free herself from Albert's sickening grasp.

"I really must find Mother," she said, glancing around wildly for any sign of the viscountess. She knew that, if her mother knew her cousin was trying to engage her, the viscountess would encourage it. But if she could get away before her cousin realized she was lying, it wouldn't matter. She would flee and hide in the gardens if she had to. Anything to get away from her horrid cousin.

Filled with desperation, she made a hasty move to escape Albert. She thought that if she could just disappear into the clusters of guests surrounding them, he would be too alcohol influenced to be able to follow her. It was a good plan, until the long, flowing train of her ballgown got caught under the feet of her drunken cousin. She didn't realize the problem until she tripped and began falling, face first, into a tall, stand supporting a large tray that was filled with crystal champagne flutes.

With a loud crash, the stand, the tray and the flutes fell to the ground. The shattering crystal echoed all throughout the ballroom, even over the sounds of the orchestra's music. The entire ballroom froze as though under a magic spell. All eyes focused on Anne and the mess at her feet, and she wished with everything in her that she could melt into the spilled champagne and broken glass that lay on the floor.

She stood, frozen in horror, her cheeks burning with humiliation. She wanted to close her eyes to block out the mess she had made, but even her eyelids were stuck. It seemed that the only thing that was capable of moving was her heart, which was pounding faster than a racing horse. And the murmurs of the guests around her that began as she tried to catch her breath did nothing to alleviate her distress.

"More of her scandalous tendencies," she heard one woman say in a tone that did little to make her think it was meant to be unheard by her.

6

"How shameful for her family," whispered a man who was just out of her line of sight to her right.

Tears stung Anne's eyes, yet not a single one of them fell. She was surprised that her cousin hadn't said a word to her in the minutes since the flutes smashed to the ground. Then, another voice rang out, not trying at all to be hushed.

"No wonder she remains unwed after two seasons," a woman with a high-pitched voice said. It was a familiar voice, but Anne couldn't bring herself to lift her head to match the face to the voice. *Won't the floor open up and swallow me to remove me from this nightmare?* She pleaded helplessly.

Naturally, no such rescue came. From the edge of her vision, she watched as her cousin, despite his previous state of inebriation, managed to slip away through the crowd, completely unnoticed in the wake of the incident that had drawn everyone's attention to her. A sob lodged itself in her throat, and she wished in a desperate moment that she could call to him, even though she could barely tolerate the sight of him. But he vanished before she could find her voice, leaving her all alone in the mess she'd made. The whispers were turning into louder, clearer admonishments and exclamations of disdain, and the room suddenly seemed too small for Anne to breathe.

Abandoning any remaining semblance of decorum, Anne turned on her heel and made a dash for the ballroom entryway. She had the presence enough of mind to gather her skirts before she took off running, thus eliminating any further trip hazard. She moved just fast enough to stun the gawking crowd, and no one tried to stop her. She succeeded in exiting the ballroom, turning blindly down the hallway that would eventually take her to the common area of her family's townhouse. She had no destination in mind, she only meant to flee the judgmental crowd of party guests. She had just gotten out of earshot of the ballroom when she began to sob, her vision blinded by hot tears.

She ran until she reached the servant's entrance that led to the gardens at the side of her family's home. She burst through the door, falling to her hands and knees onto the cool, damp grass. She cried for several moments, gripping onto the grass as though hanging on for dear life. Even though she knew it was impossible,

7

she thought she could still feel eyes boring into her. The sensation became so overwhelming that after another couple of minutes of sobbing, she had to pull herself off the ground and weave her way through the maze of hedges and rose bushes that led to the center of the gardens.

Once she was far enough away from the townhouse to shake the feeling of all those eyes on her, she finally slowed her pace. She wiped furiously at the tears streaming down her cheeks, then pressed her face into a nearby hedge full of soft, cold green leaves. The coolness of the plant offered her a miniscule comfort, and it allowed her the chance to catch her breath. She knew she would have to face her family soon enough about how horribly she had embarrassed them. But right that moment, she didn't care. In fact, if she was lucky, they would never force her to attend another social event ever again.

As she was dabbing at the last of her tears with the hem of her outer skirt, she heard a muffled cry. She held her breath, trying to identify the sound and the direction from whence it came. When she heard it again, she turned to her left, tiptoeing down the narrow path between a long row of hedges identical to the one in which she had planted her face moments before. As she walked, she noticed that the cry sounded closer, so she slowed her pace.

It took her three turns through the strategically placed rose bushes to finally locate the source of the sound. It took her a minute and some careful maneuvering to see what produced such a tiny cry. But at last, in a small sliver of crescent moonlight that shone directly beneath a bush of orange roses, she spotted a tiny, trembling bundle of dirt matted, ginger colored fur.

A little kitten, no older than three or four weeks coiled its little body, rocking sideways in a clumsy attempt to lash out at Anne. She gasped softly, the condition of the small feline melting her heart and filling her with a sudden, overwhelming sensation of protectiveness. She reached down, carefully scooping up the tiny, frail bundle of dirty fur. The kitten hissed almost inaudibly, swiping at her with a paw that was barely as big as one of Anne's fingers.

"Oh, you sweet darling," Anne cooed, cradling the kitten to her chest. "Where is your mother?"

A quick survey of the area indicated that no large cat was in sight. And from the thinness of the small animal, she guessed it hadn't nursed from its mother in a few days. She held up the kitten to get a better look at it in the moonlight. It was a boy, she realized, and he took another swipe at her nose.

Anne giggled, nuzzling the frightened creature gently with her nose. The kitten pushed on her face as she did so, issuing another hiss. But before the quiet sound had finished escaping the tiny animal's mouth, he had begun rubbing his head against her face, purring softly in her hand.

Instinctively, Anne lifted her skirt and wrapped up the little orange kitten in it. He calmed instantly, staring at Anne with curious eyes. When he mewled again, it was stronger and more insistent. Anne guessed he was hungry, and she knew she needed to find some way to fix that soon.

"It seems we're both outcasts tonight," she whispered to the kitten, her voice soft and soothing. She gently caressed the fur on his head, feeling the rapid beat of his tiny heart.

The kitten, seemingly uncertain on his feelings about her, nipped at her fingers. His razor-sharp baby teeth nicked her fingertip, but she could only giggle.

"You are a little troublemaker, aren't you?" she asked, lifting the kitten, still wrapped in her skirt, back up to the level of her eyes. "I think you shall be named Mischief."

At the sound of Anne's soft but confident proclamation of her new pet's name, the kitten tilted his head back as if to study her face. Then, he reached for her face, but not to swipe at her that time. Instead, he put his tiny paw beneath her right eye until she brought him closer to her face. Then, he put his little cold nose against her skin, beginning his purring again.

For a fleeting moment, the evening's earlier debacle faded into insignificance as Anne cradled the abandoned kitten in her arms. In the silence of the garden, Anne found solace in her newfound companion. And as he finally relented to her kindness and curled up in her arms, hiding his face with the hem of her skirt, she understood that he found solace with her, as well.

Chapter One

Anne stood staring morosely out the window, thinking about the evening ahead of her, while Martha, her loyal lady's maid, moved about with deft fingers, fastening the delicate buttons of Anne's pink gown. The dress was an artful collage of ribbons and lace, and the skirt was wide and round, exactly the way Anne loved her dresses. However, she couldn't bask in the thrill of a new, pretty dress. Dread occupied her mind and threatened to overwhelm her.

She had been surprised when her elder sister included her in the invitation to the ball she was hosting that night. After her incident at the ball the year before as she tried to escape her cousin, everyone in the ton had been reluctant to invite Anne to any events. And even though her sister was celebrating her one-year wedding anniversary with the earl of Dunbridge, Anne would have expected Elizabeth to have the same reservations about having her attend such a special event that everyone else did.

Truthfully, her peers in high society had become increasingly more hesitant to extend invitations to her, and for similar reasons. It was well known that she wasn't the most graceful lady in the ton. But even Elizabeth had been reluctant to claim a connection to her. She supposed her elder sister was obliged to invite her, along with their parents. Still, there was a nervous twist in her stomach, and she wished for a way out of attending the party. However, she knew there would be no such reprieve. Despite her clumsy escapades, and her nearing the point of being an old maid at twenty-two years of age, her parents still held a little hope that she would marry. Even if it was to her own horrid cousin.

Anne shuddered at the idea of being wed to Albert. The age difference alone between them was enough to be deemed scandalous. And his drinking habits, even outside the gentlemen's clubs, sparked rumors all over the ton. But worse of all, she would be forced to produce an heir for him, as he had never been married. As much as Anne loved the idea of having a family of her own, she could hardly stand the thought of laying, or having children, with Albert. She took a deep breath, trying to force the thoughts away.

As if sensing her need for a mood lightener, Mischief leaped onto the dressing table, swatting playfully at the ribbons on her dress. Anne laughed, reaching out for her cat with care so as to not disturb Martha while she finished with the buttons on the dress.

"My precious, we shan't play with people's clothing," she chastised, even though she found it precious when he did such things. "Do you not have enough toys to keep you occupied?"

Mischief looked up at her with his orange-yellow eyes, blinking them softly as he stretched up his neck to sniff her chin. Anne laughed again, giving the animal a kiss on the top of his head.

"I suppose that is a request for a couple of more," she said, nuzzling the ginger cat.

Mischief gently nudged her with its head until she cast her gaze upon it. Then, he meowed once, looking over his shoulder at the corner of the room, where several of the toys Anne had made for him lay scattered about.

Anne sighed, scratching the animal behind the ears.

"Very well," she said, smiling warmly at the cat. "When next I am knitting, I shall make you a new ball of yarn and make a new yarn braid for you to chew on."

Mischief blinked at her slowly again, putting his nose to her cheek as though kissing her. Then, he turned and gracefully hopped from her arms, taking up a perch on the end of the table, not far from where Anne stood.

"I suppose he means to help me dress you, Miss Anne," Martha said with a good-natured laugh as she fastened the last of the button and tied the ribbon that made a grand bow in the back of the dress.

Anne giggled again and shook her head.

"You do the most splendid work, Martha," she said. "I may loathe these parties, but I get to go to them looking my best. And that's all thanks to you."

Martha waved her hand, her pale round face flushing deep crimson.

"Speaking of parties, it's time to leave for this one," she said.

Anne took a deep breath, her emotions mingling between excitement and apprehension about attending her elder sister Elizabeth's ball. She was thrilled for her sister that she was celebrating a love that could have come right out of a storybook. Even though Elizabeth and she weren't exceptionally close, she did love her elder sister, and she wanted nothing but happiness for her. Still, she couldn't help but feel the weight of her family's expectations pressing down on her.

"Very well," she said in an airy whoosh as she exhaled the breath she had been holding. "I shall go and await the rest of the family.

Martha nodded, curtseying.

"Try to enjoy yourself this evening," she said.

Anne shrugged.

"I can pretend to try," she said.

With that, Anne descended the staircase, her skirts billowing gracefully around her. She had learned to never wear dresses with long trains, and she kept her hems as far off the ground as was considered appropriate by society. By the time she reached the first floor, Reeves, her family's butler, had materialized at the bottom of the staircase.

"Miss Anne," Reeves said, folding his tall, thin frame into a deep bow. "Your family awaits you in the carriage just outside."

Anne dipped her head and offered the kind butler a warm smile.

"Thank you, Reeves," she said.

She saw herself out, taking the moment alone to breathe and put on her best fake smile. She was miserable, but she couldn't let it show, even in her eyes. Ever since her incident with the champagne flutes the year before, her parents made it a point to watch her closely at the few events she had attended since then. The only thing more embarrassing than the whispers of the gossipers of the ton was the fact that most of them were gossiping because of the way her parents would never take their eyes off her.

The footman stepped down from his place at the rear of the coach to help her in when she approached. She gave him a silent nod of gratitude, immediately finding herself in the arms of Charlotte, her younger sister.

"Sister, you look so beautiful," she said, tugging Anne toward the seat beside her.

Anne sat beside Charlotte, grateful that her younger sister had recently debuted in society so that she could attend social events, too.

"Thank you, Char," she said, kissing her sister on the cheek. "Your purple dress looks ravishing on you."

Charlotte, who looked almost exactly like their mother with her darker red hair and lighter green eyes, blushed.

"Thank you, Anne," she said shyly. "I am so excited for tonight. I cannot wait to meet a nice gentleman that might turn out to be my husband."

Anne nodded, giving her sister a warm smile. Anne herself had little hope of marrying, especially not for love. But she was thrilled that Charlotte was hopeful and delighted with the prospect of finding love.

The viscount gave his elder daughter a firm, pointed look.

"Anne, remember the importance of proper decorum tonight," he said sternly. "We don't need any unnecessary disruptions."

He said nothing further, but the look in his eyes was clear enough. Sweet, naive Charlotte was of age to seek a match. But Anne's scandalous escapades could damage her pool of potential prospects. Deep down, Anne knew that her incident the previous year had already had an impact on Charlotte's social life. Anne cared not for the opinions of the snobs of the ton. But she did care about how her dear younger sister might be affected by any missteps on her part.

The viscountess nodded in agreement with her husband. Her eyes were softer, but only marginally, and Anne felt sure it was only because Charlotte was present.

"Please, darling, do not let us down," she said.

Anne cheeks reddened, but she nodded. The invisible weight she was carrying on her shoulders grew heavier, and she wanted to leap out of the carriage, even though it was now moving. Instead, she fixed her gaze outside the window, fighting to keep her composure. She knew she had to remain calm, even though she wanted to say something in her own defense. It always seemed as though her parents missed the things that led up to one of her so-called disruptions. Like the rest of society, they only seemed to see her acting out and accidents. But in her twenty-two years, she had learned to not try to speak up. Women were expect to be compliant and silent, no matter what the situation was.

"Mother, Father," Charlotte said, sounding offended. "Don't be so hard on Anne. She is a wonderful young woman, and she never means to cause trouble."

Anne looked at her younger sister, giving her a small, grateful smile. Charlotte was the sweetest young lady Anne had ever known. She thought again about how her antics were hurting her little sister, and she vowed silently that she would be on her best behavior that night, no matter what, if only for Charlotte's sake.

The viscount and viscountess said nothing, but they exchanged a silent look. Anne blushed again, but she kept her eyes on her sister.

"It's all right," she said. "Tonight will be a wonderful night for us all. You'll see."

About half an hour later, the Huxley family arrived at Dunbridge Manor. Anne's heart quickened as she stepped out of the carriage. Elizabeth and her husband, James Ashford, stood at the door of the mansion, their smiles shining brilliantly in the fading evening sun.

"I am so glad you all came," Elizabeth said, embracing first her parents and then her youngest sister.

"Thank you all for coming," James said, bowing as he, too, greeted the Huxley's. As James and the viscount shook hands and exchanged mild pleasantries, Elizabeth reluctantly embraced Anne.

"How are you, Sister?" she asked, her voice carrying the same wariness that her parents' had.

Anne tried to smile, but she knew it was more of a grimace.

"I am well, thank you," she mumbled, not surprised when Elizabeth turned back to their parents before she had finished her response.

"Please, come in," she said. "The rest of the guests should arrive any moment."

Anne and her family followed her elder sister and the earl to the ballroom, which was the epitome of grandeur, with chandeliers casting shimmering light upon the crowd of guests who mingled on the fringes of the dance floor. Anne's eyes immediately found her dearest friend of two years, Susan, at the opposite end of the room. Susan spotted Anne in the same instant, and she waved merrily at her, motioning her over.

"Excuse me, Mother," Anne said, pausing long enough to give Charlotte a brief kiss on the cheek. "Susan is calling to me."

Without waiting for a response and hoping to slip out of her mother's line of vision in the crowd, Anne vanished, making her way toward Susan. Her dear friend met her halfway, rushing up to her and throwing her arms around Anne.

"I am so glad to see you," Susan said, beaming at Anne. "Come and talk with me. Tell me how you've been lately."

Anne laughed as Susan dragged her to the refreshment tables, which were arranged vertically along the back wall of the ballroom. Susan fetched two glasses of wine, handing one to Anne, which she took gratefully.

"It is good to see you, too, Susan," she said. "Mother and Father made sure to embarrass me quite nicely on the way here."

Susan sighed, shaking her head.

"Are they still upset about last year?" she asked.

Anne nodded.

"And the dinner party where I discreetly admonished the overly forward baron with a gentle tap to his shin beneath the table," she said, unable to help smiling at the memory. "And the ball where I 'accidentally' stomped the drunk earl's foot when his hand 'accidentally' slipped down my back."

Susan rolled her eyes, shaking her head.

"They should be grateful that you would not subject yourself to such inappropriate behaviour," she said. "One would think that would reflect more on your character than you defending yourself."

Anne nodded, taking a generous drink of her wine.

"One would think," she murmured.

Susan gave her a sympathetic look.

"Well, don't you worry, my dearest," she said. "You and I shall remain in each other's company this evening. I will never be too far away."

But no sooner than she had spoken the words than a gentleman in a crisp green suit approached. Anne took a step back, knowing full well he hadn't come to speak to her. Her instincts proved right when he completely ignored her and held out his hand to Susan.

"May I have your first dance, Lady Susan?" he asked.

Susan looked at Anne over her shoulder, looking torn. Anne gave her a reassuring smile, subtly waving her toward the dance floor. After a moment of hesitation, Susan reluctantly turned to face the gentleman.

"Of course," she said, looking back at Anne once more. "I will be right back," she mouthed before allowing the gentleman to lead her onto the dance floor.

Anne remained alone near the refreshment table, finishing her first glass of wine, and reaching for another. She knew she should pace herself, as she could hardly afford to get too lightheaded from the wine and end up on the dance floor. But deep down, she knew that she wouldn't be asked for a dance. And when the first strains of the first dance set of the evening wafted from the orchestra and she still stood alone, she was hardly surprised.

Her thoughts were just beginning to wander and she was preparing for another evening of staying as hidden as possible and doing her best to avoid trouble when Lord Sebastian Gray, the only person in the ton more notorious for his mischief than she was for hers, sauntered over to her. Anne froze, not daring to so much as blink, lest she manage to blind herself just enough to trip herself. Or Lord Gray.

"I see that you are as popular as ever on the dance floor," he said with a snicker. "I do hope your feet aren't too sore by the end of the night."

Anne's blood heated instantly, and she turned her face away from him. She wanted to push away the insolent man, but she remembered her promise to herself to not embarrass Charlotte.

"I see that you're not dancing, either," she retorted, smiling smugly.

Lord Gray chuckled, purposely bumping into the hand with which she held her wine glass as he reached around her to fetch his own. She managed to keep her grip, but just barely, and her temper rose a few centimeters.

"It is by choice, I assure you," he said. "I had an important business conversation to finish, and then I felt compelled to pay my respects and offer salutations. But I knew I would have plenty of time for that, seeing as how no one would dare risk dancing with the most impudent lady in the ton."

Anne's vision went red and, before she could think better of it, she threw her glass of wine at him. The red liquid coated the white cravat of Lord Gray's immaculately tailored suit, and the glass tumbled to the floor with a loud thud. It didn't shatter, but that made no difference. Several people had witnessed her tantrum and soon enough, everyone was once more staring at her.

As at the ball the previous year, the ballroom fell completely silent. Her heart pounded wildly in her chest as she stared out at the faces that were rapidly filling with shock and disapproval. She had certainly caused a disruption, just as her family had feared. To make matters worse, people were coming up and offering Lord Gray, who was feigning shock and ignorance, assistance in getting the wine off his suit. Would there ever be an end to the embarrassing injustices Anne kept seeming to encounter?

Chapter Two

Richard Stratford, the duke of Calder, walked into the softly lit gentleman's club, White's, grateful for the respite from the constant demands of his title and mindless gossip and unreasonable expectations of London's elite on noblemen. Floating wafts of cigar smoke and the fragrance of polished wood greeted him like an old friend, helping him to forget the pressures and tediousness of day-to-day life. The times when he could sneak away alone were precious to him. They were the only reason why he could keep pressing on with his life as a duke.

He habitually glanced casually around, noting a few familiar faces amongst the pairs and small groups of men placing bets at card games, playing billiards and sitting and talking quietly to one another. But one face in particular caught his attention, and he smiled at once. Seated at their usual table was Thomas Harville, his closest friend, sipping on a glass of whiskey. It was a happy coincidence to see his friend there, so he made his way over to him. He waved to one of the waiters who recognized him as one of the club's regulars, to which the waiter nodded and disappeared behind the bar, no spoken words needed.

"Richard," Thomas said, greeting him with a warm smile. "You've been scarce of late. I hope all is well with you."

Richard chuckled wryly as he took a seat opposite his friend.

"All is as well as ever, Thomas," he said, avoiding his friend's gaze. That wasn't entirely true. But he didn't want to spend this unexpected time with his friend discussing his problems.

Thomas was never one to be fooled, however. He studied Richard carefully, locking eyes with him as he sipped his drink.

"Far be it from me to debate a man on his feelings," he said. "But I must say that I don't quite believe you. Are you sure you are doing well?"

Richard sighed, giving his friend a sheepish smile.

"You were never one to be deceived," he said, feeling resigned. "I have been keeping busy with business affairs and trips out of town to prevent Mother from interfering in my life."

Thomas raised his eyebrow, opening his mouth to speak but being silenced by the arrival of Richard's drink. After Richard tipped the waiter, Thomas tried again.

"What is she doing to meddle with your life?" he asked.

Richard finished half his drink in one gulp, wincing at the burn of the bourbon.

"She persists that I must marry and prepare to sire an heir to the dukedom of Calder," he said, rolling his eyes. "Worst still, she keeps trying to choose my bride."

Thomas nodded thoughtfully, but he finished his drink without saying a word. After a long moment of silence, Thomas gently smacked the table with his palm and grinned at Richard.

"How about a game of billiards?" he asked.

Richard smiled, albeit warily. It wasn't like Thomas to change the subject during a conversation unless he was thinking about what was said and had something to say on the subject. Still, it had been ages since Richard played billiards, and it sounded like a nice reprieve from dwelling in his thoughts about his mother's matchmaking efforts alone.

He followed Thomas to the gaming room where the billiard tables were lined up neatly in well-spaced-out rows. There were two tables available, and Thomas led them to the one at the far back of the room. He racked the balls, setting up the game while Richard selected sticks with which they could play. Richard took the first shot, but all the while he could feel his friend's eyes on him. After his first ball missed its target, he looked up to find Thomas staring at him with the same thoughtful expression he'd had at the table. He took his own shot, sinking his first ball and securing the striped balls for that round of the game, missing the second. Then, he looked at Richard and sighed.

"My friend, you can't keep avoiding marriage forever," he said. "Perhaps there is something to the thought of you settling down."

Richard raised his eyebrows at his friend as though Thomas had suggested that he walk off the pier with a full suit of armor on.

"Has mother gotten to you, too?" he asked. He jested, but he wondered at his friend's sudden agreement with such an abstract notion. Richard had never been one for the idea of

20

marriage, and Thomas was well aware of that fact. What would make his friend think he would change his mind now?

Thomas nodded, giving a small smile as he held up one hand.

"I do not mean to offend," he said. "But consider this. If you took it upon yourself to find a bride of your choosing, perhaps it would put an end to your mother's meddling."

Richard blinked, surprised by his friend's logic. He still didn't think he could bring himself to consider the possibility of marriage right then. But nor could he deny that Thomas had a point. If he were to lose his mind and decide to marry, he would rather it be a woman he chose to wed, not one of the many shallow, air-headed heiresses his mother kept pushing on him.

As Richard lined up a shot, he considered Thomas's words. Could choosing his own candidate for marriage be his escape from his mother's incessant scheming? He didn't imagine that she would be too thrilled with him for rejecting the women she wanted him to consider courting.

"I think that Mother might be more furious with me for such an effort," he said, voicing his thoughts.

Thomas chuckled.

"I think you are right," he said. "But by all accounts, you would still be doing what she wants you to do. And she could hardly bicker with you for doing what she's been pressing upon you for so long."

Richard shook his head, making the shot he had just taken. He made two more shots before missing again, looking at his friend doubtfully.

"I must say that I can't be any more enthusiastic about your suggestion than I am about Mother's pestering," he said. "How can I find a bride when a bride is the last thing that I want?"

Thomas shrugged, eyeing the table for his next shot before speaking again.

"No one could expect you to embrace the notion immediately," he said. "Just take some time to consider it. Surely, if you kept in mind that you are doing this to keep control of your own life, you could keep an eye out for a lady that piques your interest. Even if it takes you the rest of the season, it should appease your mother than you are taking some initiative in finding yourself a wife."

Richard shuddered at Thomas's last word as his friend took his shot. Thomas must have seen the movement, as he laughed and scratched the cue against the table, barely bunting his ball from its spot on the green material.

"I do not mean to laugh at your plight," Thomas said, despite continuing to laugh. "I am just surprised by how reluctant you seem toward marriage."

Richard nodded, leaning on the stick he held in his hand.

"I am sure it sounds strange," he said. "We are all taught from a young age that we grow up, we marry, we have children, we care for our families and then we pass on. And I am aware that I owe my family's dukedom an heir. But having a wife seems like more of a hindrance to me than an asset."

Thomas frowned, tilting his head.

"Do you mean to say that you do not believe in love?" he asked.

Richard shrugged.

"I do not judge those who claim to have found love," he said. "How could I possibly cherish a lady devoid of intellect and personality, akin to a faded sofa cushion?"

Thomas burst out laughing, slapping his knee as Richard smirked.

"That is true enough," he said, wiping at the corners of his eyes. "But what if there was a woman out there who had a little more personality and intellect than that?"

Richard snorted.

"Then it would be only a little more," he said. "And that would be a miracle that even the heavens likely couldn't deliver."

The two men shared a laugh, and Richard relaxed a bit with the humorous interlude. Then, Thomas nodded, straightening his coat and shaking his head.

"I think that no man could suffer a woman such as you described for long periods of time," he said. "But I think that you could find a woman who could offer that which you seek."

Richard sighed again, shaking his head.

"But what I seek is an escape from marriage," he said. "I can't find that and find a wife simultaneously."

Thomas shook his head.

"No," he said. "But you mustn't rule out the idea of picking a woman you could tolerate for the rest of your life. We both know that your mother will never relent. And it isn't as if you need to make up your mind this instant. Just think about it, my friend. It can't be any worse than what your mother will undoubtedly deliver to you if you don't take control of the situation."

Richard nodded slowly as Thomas's words continued to sink in. He knew that his friend was right. There was nothing that would get him out of a marriage to some noblewoman, short of him fleeing London, and thus, his responsibilities as duke. And his dukedom was something he took very seriously, so running away was out of the question. He would never desire marriage. But if he didn't want to guarantee his own misery for the rest of his days, he knew he should do something to take charge of his own decisions in the matter.

"I'll consider it," Richard finally conceded, sinking a ball with a soft thud. "But I am placing a bet right now that I could never find a woman I believe to be worth more than five minutes of my time."

Thomas raised his eyebrows in intrigue.

"Is that a money-worthy wager?" he asked.

Richard snickered.

"I'll tell you what," he said jovially. "If I find a woman worth marrying by the end of this season, I will pay your membership dues here for the next ten years."

Thomas laughed heartily again and nodded.

"I am happy to take that bet," he said.

Richard offered his hand, feeling confident in his side of the wager.

"Consider the wager made, my friend," he said.

Thomas nodded, pausing just long enough to take another shot. Richard noticed there were only five balls left on the table. Thomas righted himself after making one shot but missing the next. He held out his stick in front of him, leaning his hip against the billiard table.

"So, to whom is your mother trying to marry you this week?" he asked with a grin.

Richard groaned at the thought.

"Lady Eleanor Westbrook," he said.

Thomas gaped at Richard, slowly shaking his head.

"Well, I can see why you would be reluctant about her," he said. "There is no greater sofa cushion in all of London."

Richard snorted, but it was a statement too close to the truth for him to find any true humor.

"She is as rigid as they come," he said. "She reminds me quite a bit of Mother, now that I think of it."

Thomas sniffed.

"That would explain why your mother would suggest her," he said.

Richard shuddered again.

"Let's forget about that," he said. "I have a game to win."

Thomas laughed once more, looking at Richard with bemusement.

"I believe it is I who will win," he said.

Thomas was right. He did, indeed, with that round of billiards. The gentlemen concluded their refreshments and requested additional libations before Richard proceeded to set up the following round. Thomas kept Richard in high spirits by discussing his new business ventures in the perfume and cosmetic industry and the fresh connections the trade opened up to him. It was a relief to Richard to finally be able to forget his mother's meddling for a little while. He drank and played his troubles away with Thomas until well into the evening. Despite the darkening sky outside the windows of the club, he was disappointed when Thomas walked over to the wall and replaced his billiard cue stick.

"I believe I will take my leave," he said. "I have an early meeting with Lord Harton in the morning. We will be arranging our first shipment of cosmetics, hopefully for next week."

Richard nodded, clapping his friend on the back.

"Good luck to you, my friend," he said. "I do hope we can do this again soon."

Thomas grinned and nodded.

"I will take any chance I can get to beat you at billiards," he said.

The cool night air caressed Richard's face as he stepped outside the club. He waved farewell to Thomas, then took his time taking the short walk to his waiting carriage. It was a pleasant night, and Richard wished he had walked to the club. Thomas's words echoed in his thoughts, and once again, he found himself seeing sense in the idea his friend had proposed. Could he really shape his own future on his own terms? Was it truly so simple?

Chapter Three

Anne felt as though she had stones tied to her limbs when she awoke the next morning. It was all she could do to sit upright in bed and pull the cord to summon Martha. As soon as she had, she buried her face in her hands, wishing that, as she used to pretend when she was a child, it would make her invisible. She wanted to cry, but no tears came. The burden of the humiliation from the previous evening was too heavy on her heart, and she had cried out every last teardrop before falling into a restless, uncomfortable sleep.

When Martha entered, Anne quietly pushed herself out of bed, walking dutifully to her dressing area and waiting for her lady's maid to select a dress. By the time Martha reached her, ready to dress her for the day, she had noticed Anne's dour mood. She draped the outfit over one arm and gently squeezed Anne's shoulder with her free hand.

"Miss Anne, why do you look so troubled?" she asked.

Anne sighed, quickly filling Martha in on the incident with Lord Gray. Martha pulled her into a tight embrace, giving her a gentle smile.

"Well, who could blame you for throwing wine in his face after that?" she asked.

Anne chortled, her eyes burning as if with tears, but once again, none came.

"The entirety of the ton, it seems," she mumbled.

Martha shook her head, carefully lifting Anne's arms so she could pull her mistress's night dress over her head.

"What do those uptight, snobby fools know?" she asked.

Anne tried to smile, as she agreed with her lady's maid. But she couldn't quite manage. Instead, she shrugged, shaking her head.

"They know enough to stir up Mother and Father with their shaming of me," she said. "It's not fair. I shouldn't have to take such abuse from such a despicable man, even if it's unladylike to defend myself. Why should he get away with saying such cruel things without so much as a reprimand?"

Martha shook her head, giving Anne a sympathetic look.

"He shouldn't," she said. "I am well aware that you must experience deep humiliation, particularly in light of those unfeeling individuals spreading baseless gossip about it. But you did the right thing. And I bet he will think twice before crossing you like that again."

Anne nodded, biting back her dubiousness. If anything, the previous night had likely given him, and other men like him, more of a reason to pick at her. It would certainly place her at the center of gossip in the ladies' circles. And the worst part of all was that Charlotte would pay the price for her actions.

As Martha pulled the blue gown over her head, she considered crawling back into bed and feigning an illness. But she knew that would only enrage her parents even more if she tried to avoid them after such a debacle.

"Are you ready, Miss Anne?" Martha asked, gesturing toward the door.

Anne shook her head, sighing heavily.

"Not at all," she said. "But I suppose I have no choice."

Martha shook her head, smiling sadly at Anne.

"I should say not," she said. "Your parents would likely drag you out of your chambers."

Anne smiled at her lady's maid's delightful jest. But deep down, she believed that wasn't too far from the truth. She straightened her shoulders, determined to hold her head as high as possible. Whatever wrath was coming from her parents, she would take it with silent grace. Then, as soon as she was able, she would sneak away to the gardens to play with Mischief for a while.

Slowly, but with determination, Anne forced her feet to carry her to the drawing room. She heard the hushed murmuring as she reached the door, and she was not at all surprised when three pairs of eyes immediately turned to her. Her father's burned with barely contained anger, her mother's reflected shame and apparent anguish, and Charlotte's were filled with concern and sympathy.

Anne's heart broke. No matter how grievously her endeavours wounded her younger sibling, Charlotte never held her accountable. She offered Anne a weak smile as she walked over to the table to join her family. Anne gave one back, wishing she could apologize to her younger sister. She took her seat, arranging her skirts with deliberate composure, despite the churning of her anxious stomach. Her parents were seated across from her, their expressions seemingly frozen on their faces.

It didn't take Anne long to see why neither of her parents had spoken a word since she entered the room. The newspaper lay on the table, sprawled across her father's empty plate, and the scandal sheet was facing the ceiling. Anne glanced at Charlotte, who gave her a sympathetic nod. Anne swallowed, reluctantly lifting her head, and bracing herself for what she knew was to come.

"Anne," her father said, his voice clipped and sharp as he gestured towards the newspaper. "As usual, your behaviour at the ball has not gone unnoticed. Why you can never keep yourself out of trouble is something I will never understand. I hope you are proud of yourself. That would make one of us at this table who is."

Anne flinched at the harshness of her father's last sentence.

"You don't understand, Father," she said, trying to plead her case. "He said something very cruel to me, with the intention of hurting and upsetting me. I reacted without thinking."

Her mother sighed, pointing firmly at the scandal sheet.

"That's the problem," she said, her words just as biting as the viscount's had been. "You do not think. You humiliate this family repeatedly, and you never think about how that reflects on us."

Anne's heart sank as she followed her mother's finger along the bold, black headline.

Miss Anne Huxley Takes Center Stage Again by Ruining Another Ball.

Anne scanned the story, flushing deeply as she read a detailed account of her confrontation with Lord Gray. Once more, she found a complete lack of shock when the author of the article named her a 'reckless aggressor,' and Lord Gray an innocent victim in what was just considered to be Anne's latest public display of unladylike behavior.

Anne shook her head, frustration blending with the shame she felt.

"I don't think it's fair that the ton would judge things that are ultimately harmless," she said, struggling to not whine. "No one is ever hurt. And it isn't as though I am risking my reputation with anything I do."

Her father chortled.

"No, of course not," he said sarcastically. "You are only risking Charlotte's reputation.

The breakfast table felt like a tribunal with the heavy atmosphere and her parents' disapproving glares judging her every move. In her nervous trembling, she nearly knocked over her water glass. Both her parents sighed in unison with clear agitation. Charlotte tried to comfort Anne by gently patting her back. But Anne was inconsolable. She just prayed for the tongue lashing to end so that she could hide in her chambers until she was ready to come out. Which, the way she felt right then, likely wouldn't be until she died.

"Anne, you've tarnished our family's name," she said. "For a couple of years, we had the fortune of being able to explain away your behaviour as the indiscretions of a young, unseasoned woman. But now, you are nearly an old maid. You know better, and you still act like a teenage girl. The whole ton is condemning our family, and we only have you to blame."

Anne bit her lip and lowered her head. Her head was pounding in time with her heart, giving her the megrim that she had wished for before coming down for breakfast.

"Your father and I have been talking, Daughter," the viscountess said, her voice no warmer than the lakes during Christmastide. "We agree that your actions must now have consequences. This cannot continue. We will not allow you to ruin Charlotte's life because you cannot behave like a proper lady."

Anne dared to glance at her father, whose expression was at last changing. Instead of the bitter scowl, he was now almost smirking. Something in his eyes made her stomach flip, and she had to sip her water to keep the bile from rising in her throat.

The viscount held up his own glass toward his middle daughter, glancing down at the paper before locking eyes with Anne once again.

"To restore our good name, you will marry Albert," he said.

A knot tightened in Anne's stomach at the mention of her distant cousin's name. She looked to her mother for help, but she quickly saw there would be none. The viscountess gave her a look that told Anne she was satisfied with the decision that had been reached. She shook her head, trying to protest against the idea of marrying a man as insufferable as Albert.

"Albert has, fortunately, had an interest in you for some time," the viscountess said, looking relieved. "It is the best course of action to prevent any future incidents that could harm Charlotte or leave us in the center of any more gossip within the ton. That Albert is willing to risk taking on that burden is certainly a stroke of luck."

Anne dropped her head as her hopes for escaping the advances of her dreadful cousin crumbled. She had once believed that her parents would protect her, at least from a marriage to a cousin who did little but drink and create his own rumors and was twice her age. But the harsh reality became painfully clear.

"Surely, this won't be necessary," Anne whispered, knowing full well there was no point in pressing the issue.

Sure enough, her father pretended as though she hadn't spoken.

"Albert and I have already discussed the matter," he said. "He said that once we had reached our decision, he would have the arrangements made for the two of you to wed when he returns from his last business trip."

Anne stared dumbly ahead, her thoughts screaming but her voice too weak to use. Beside her, Charlotte remained silent, but her concern was almost tangible enough to touch. She silently reached out and put her hand over Anne's. Only then could Anne turn to give her sister another faint smile.

"Very well," she said, her voice breaking with the strain of speaking through her dread. "May I be excused?"

Without waiting for an answer, she gave Charlotte one more tight smile, then exited the room without another word. She ran all the way back up the stairs, tumbling through the door to her bedchambers so quickly that she woke Mischief from his slumber. The cat raised from his soft, plush bed, stretching his muscular body across the floor as he made his way to his mistress. Anne bent down to scratch him behind the ears as he rubbed himself against her legs.

"Oh, Mischief," she said, surprising even herself at how mournful she sounded. "How did my life come to this?"

The ginger cat tilted his head up to look at her, blinking slowly before licking her hand, which dangled limply at her side. Anne scratched him again, wandering aimlessly over to her desk. One idea, bleak and useless as she was sure it was, came to her. She pulled out some stationery and her pen quill as Mischief curled up at her feet. As quickly as her trembling hands would allow, she penned a letter to Susan, pleading with her friend for the chance to speak with her.

She briefly explained the pending wedding plans, begging Susan to visit her as soon as she could. Then, she sealed the letter, sending up a silent prayer. Susan might not have a solution for her. But perhaps, if she could talk things over with the one person to whom she felt closest apart from Charlotte, things wouldn't seem so hopeless and frightening. At the very least, it would give her something to look forward to before her life was turned upside down.

Chapter Four

A knock on his bedchamber door roused Richard from a deep, alcohol assisted slumber. He sat up, rubbing his eyes to clear them of the sleep from whence he had just been dragged.

"Enter," he boomed, his voice thick with fatigue.

Watson, his valet, strode into the room, a look of purpose on his face.

"Her Grace insisted that I come fetch you at once," he said. "She said she wishes to discuss something with you straightaway."

Richard groaned. He didn't need to ask what she wanted. It didn't take a scholar to guess what she would say to him. She spoke of him finding a bride every day as of late, and she would continue to do so until he was finally wed. But why had she had him awoken? Usually, she waited until he joined her for a meal to begin her meddling. What changed that morning?

Still groggy, Richard shook his head at the unspoken question. It didn't matter. He would get up and get dressed and face his mother. Perhaps, if he could get the pesky conversation out of the way early that day, he could spend the rest of the day avoiding her without incurring her wrath.

He padded over to his dresser, blindly pulling out a fancy blue suit and matching boots. He had no plans for the day, as he had completed all his ledgers for the month just two days prior and wouldn't need to begin the new ones for another day or so. But he thought that, if his mother became too persistent, he might steal away to White's again.

"Don't be of too much help, milord," Watson said wryly as he tugged on Richard's arm.

Richard glanced down and realized that he had been standing immobile while the valet tried to help him dress. He smirked despite himself at Watson's sarcastic humor. His valet wasn't one for mincing words, and despite his dry wit, he was respectful and loyal to Richard.

"Forgive me," he said. "I suppose my arms feel as heavy as my mind does."

Watson snorted as Richard held out his arms.

"A few too many spirits last night, milord?" he quipped.

Richard chuckled.

"Not quite enough, I'm afraid," he said.

Watson joined in the soft laughter.

"I can imagine your mother would be most thrilled with an inebriated duke first thing in the morning," he said.

Richard shrugged.

"She can add that to the list of things I do that displease her, I suppose," he said.

Watson laughed more heartily. Then, he set to work, quickly dressing his master. When he was finished, Richard ran a hand through his hair haphazardly, fetching a blue top hat from the rack behind the door to his chambers. He placed the hat atop his head, not caring to bother with the routine of combing and styling his hair.

Watson frowned, shaking his head.

"The intricacies that manifest in your hair are sufficient to occupy an entire day," he said dryly.

Richard chuckled once more.

"I shall brush them out for you, Watson," he said. "For now, I must go see what Mother wants."

Watson bowed, whisking himself to the door to open it for his master.

"I'm only a summons away, milord," he said, sounding playfully less than enthusiastic at the prospect of Richard calling for him again.

Richard smirked and nodded.

"You needn't worry," he said. "I expect to leave immediately after breakfast this morning."

With that, Richard took a deep breath, practicing the same bland expression he had been learning to perfect whenever his mother spoke of marriage. He descended the stairs between the third and second floors, and then the grand staircase that led out into the grand hall of Calder Manor. It was oddly silent, as he was accustomed to hearing chatter coming from the drawing room during breakfast. Coupled with his mother's intentional summons for him before he had awoken, he couldn't help thinking that something was amiss.

As Richard entered the drawing room, he was immediately stricken by a heavy, suffocating cloud of invisible tension that hung in the air. Susan looked notably distressed, her brow furrowed as she looked at her brother. His mother sat in a high-backed chair, her gaze fixed upon the newspaper, which lay splayed out in front of her on the table.

With a quick glance, Richard noticed that it was open to the latest edition of the scandal sheets, and that his mother was studying it with a look of concentrated distaste. He had no idea what would have so heavily earned her disapproval. But he was certain that it was of no consequence to him. Still, he had the distinct that it was about to become something into which he was dragged. He took his seat, settling in for what was to come.

"Good morning," he said, trying to sound as though he wasn't aware of the strained atmosphere in the room.

Adelaide Stratford looked up from the newspaper with a sigh.

"Richard, my dear," she said, her tone stern. "Forgive my distractedness. I was just reading about Miss Anne Huxley's escapade at the ball last night."

Richard frowned, thinking back to the ball. He had attended with his mother and sister, but he couldn't recall any incident that was noteworthy. Of course, not long after the ball began, he had slipped outside into the gardens, opting to hide away from the party. He couldn't tell his mother that, however. Instead, he gave her a vague smile.

"Oh?" he asked. "What do the scandal sheets have to say about it?"

His mother didn't seem to notice his ignorance. She shook her head, lifting the paper idly before letting it fall back down onto the table.

"Throwing wine in the face of a gentleman who undoubtedly merely went to ask her for a dance," she said, clucking her tongue. "The scandal sheets rightfully expose her for being the scandalous, unladylike human being she is. It is no wonder the lady is still unmarried after two full seasons since her debut."

Richard bit his tongue, trying not to laugh. He had to admit that the image of a ton lady throwing wine on a stuffy gentleman was entertaining to him. Part of him wished that he hadn't absconded from the ball. He thought that would have been a nice change from the predictable sequence of the stages of a typical ton party.

"Mother," Susan said, almost pleading. "I really think the paper is blowing things all out of proportion. I know Anne very well, and I do not think she would do such a thing if not for a very good reason."

Richard looked at his sister, surprised at her for standing up to their mother. He knew Miss Huxley and she were good friends. But Susan had never been one for disobedience when it came to their mother. He watched, waiting to see what the dowager duchess would say to her defiant daughter.

The dowager merely sighed, pointing to the paper with another click of her tongue.

"Susan," she said, "I am rather concerned about your friendship with this lady. She is hardly the kind of company to keep if you wish to protect your reputation. As you can see, the ton frowns upon ladies who behave in such a manner. To be associated with her could mean that you are considered to be as unladylike and uncouth as she is."

Susan scowled at their mother, shaking her head.

"You are being most unfair, Mother," she said. "Anne is the sweetest woman you could ever know. People judge her without learning why she does the things she does. I think it would be worse if she were known for being too friendly with men."

The dowager gave her daughter an indulgently sympathetic look.

"My precious, you do not understand how society works," she said. "If a young lady cannot be polite and proper in public, she might as well be married to five men at once. Miss Huxley is a blight on society, and I would rather not see you get any more mixed up with her than you already are."

Susan looked as though she wanted to say something else, and Richard could see in her eyes that it would be less than flattering to the dowager. But she silenced herself, staring down at her plate still filled with food, her cheeks red and her chest rising and falling rapidly with her apparent irritation.

Richard looked at his mother, feeling protective of his younger sister.

"Mother, don't you think that's enough of the nonsense scandal sheets for today?" he asked.

The dowager duchess looked at him as though she wanted to say something more about the incident from the night before. But she glanced at the clock and her expression changed, and she looked at Richard with a look in her eyes that he was all too familiar with.

"Your concern needs to be with Eleanor today," she said. "Her mother and she will be joining us for tea at any moment. I want to remind you of how important it is that you are present when they arrive. You can hardly make an impression on Victoria if you are off gallivanting in town."

Richard bit the inside of his cheek, stifling a sigh. He thought back to his conversation with Thomas about the young lady. She was, by all accounts, very prim and proper, much like his mother. However, when eyes were off of her, she had a tendency to make her interest in Richard very blatantly and forwardly known. It was as uncomfortable for him as her strict, proper attitude in front of others. He had known that his mother was pressing for him to consider marrying her. But now, it seemed as though she intended to ensure a match between the two of them, no matter what Richard thought.

"I understand, Mother," he said, his disinterest clear as he spoke.

His mother's eyes bore into his, and she gave him a stern gaze as though she picked up on his reluctance.

"Good," she said. "You have no way out of this obligation, Richard. You must make an effort to be agreeable."

Richard chewed his tongue to hold back his true response. He might have no way out of such an obligation. But he had no intention of making himself agreeable. If his mother wanted to match him with Lady Eleanor, he would make it as difficult as possible for her.

36

He didn't get much time to consider how he would rebuke the young lady's affections, however. The butler entered, with Lady Eleanor and her mother right on his heels. His mother rose, shoving the paper aside quickly as she greeted her friend and her daughter. Susan grabbed the paper and folded it up, tucking it beside her in her chair. Richard could see that his sister was deep in thought. But he didn't get a chance to see about her because their mother cleared her throat and ushered Lady Eleanor over to him.

"Please, have a seat," she cooed, giving Richard another stern look. "You remember my son, Richard."

Lady Eleanor curtseyed primly, her blond curls bouncing lightly as she did so. She looked the part of the proper young lady, but when her eyes met Richard's, they glinted with something akin to hunger. Richard stood and bowed, pointedly taking a seat in a solitary chair, rather than sitting back down on the sofa where he had been sitting.

"Please, take a comfortable seat," he said with exaggerated sweetness, looking at Lady Eleanor and her mother as he gestured to the sofa.

The three women standing looked displeased, but none of them said anything. Their guests complied, sitting on the sofa as the servants poured them tea and served the cakes. Richard glanced at the clock, noticing that it was just past noon. It was sure to be a long day, and he hoped that Lady Eleanor and her mother wouldn't stay long.

Tea was every bit as oppressive as Richard had imagined it would be. He kept to himself, only offering noncommittal nods and murmurs when he was forced to do so. Lady Eleanor's determined pursuit of his attention was quite conspicuous, and her mother, Lady Victoria seemed equally eager to engage him in conversation.

The combination of Eleanor, Victoria, and his mother made the room's environment even more suffocating than it had been when he first entered while his mother was reading the scandal sheets. He could feel his mother's ice-cold glare on him each time he refused to respond to any of the conversation topics. That was fine with him. His mother had said he needed to be present. She hadn't said he needed to be charming. It was a childish mentality, he knew. But as far as he was concerned, so was his mother's matchmaking attempts. Perhaps, she would finally learn to stop doing that to him.

His thoughts drifted again to his conversation with Thomas. It was becoming clear that, if he wanted to silence his mother permanently on the subject of him taking a wife, he would have to take matters into his own hands. But where would he begin his search for a bride? And how could he ever expect to find a woman who wasn't just as bad as Lady Eleanor?

His mother cleared her throat loudly, drawing his attention to her. The ice in her eyes was evident, despite the wide smile on her face. She looked at him in a way that made Richard uncomfortable. She was up to something. And he was sure he didn't want to know what it was.

"Richard, my dear," she crooned, holding his gaze firmly. "Why don't you accompany Eleanor on a carriage ride to Rotton Park?"

Richard had to act quickly to keep his mouth from falling open. He might have expected such a request from Lady Eleanor herself. But his mother was a picture of propriety and primness. For her to make such a forward suggestion when it was up to the gentlemen to extend such invitations was as shocking as it was repulsive to him. His cheeks grew warm, not from embarrassment, but from anger, and he tried to collect his thoughts to think of some excuse to reject the trip. But to his relief, Susan rose, moving closer to Richard and breaking the eye contact he held with their mother. She gave him a pointed look before turning to their mother, offering an apologetic smile.

"Forgive me, Mother," Susan said, her voice steady. "But did you forget that Richard and I have a prearranged trip to the library this afternoon?"

Richard couldn't hide his surprise at Susan's sudden intervention. He knew no such plans had been made, but he played along, offering his sister a grateful smile.

The dowager duchess's lips pressed into a thin line.

"I can't say that I recall that discussion," she said, her agitation barely suppressed beneath more of the fake sweetness with which she had spoken to Richard. "Are you certain that's today?"

Susan nodded, clasping her hands in front of her.

"Yes," she said. "I have been looking forward to this for days. And I can hardly go without a proper chaperone."

The dowager glanced at Richard, who nodded silently along with his sister. At last, she sighed, giving Lady Eleanor and Lady Victoria an apologetic smile.

"I suppose the ride can wait for another day," she said.

Susan curtseyed to their guests, prompting Richard to bow. He offered the falsest sheepish smile he had ever given, hoping his relief didn't show too clearly in his eyes.

"Forgive me, ladies," he said softly. "We really must be off now."

Without waiting for a response from any of the women, Richard offered his sister his arm and they hurried out of the drawing room. They rushed outside, both of them seeming equally convinced that their mother might try to follow them and question them about the fake trip to town.

Once they were seated in the carriage, which was thankfully ready for a trip, Richard looked at his sister with bewilderment.

"Thank you for intervening, Sister," he said.

Susan smiled warmly.

"Anything to spare you from another of Eleanor's horrid advances," she said.

Richard chuckled softly, appreciating his sister's understanding. However, his gratitude was short-lived when Susan leaned in closer with a sheepish expression on her face.

"We're not going to the library," she said. "We're going to the Huxley residence."

Richard raised an eyebrow in surprise.

"Why would you take me there?" he asked.

Susan shrugged, but she would no longer meet his eyes.

"I've been meaning to visit Anne lately," she said. "And since you are already escorting me someplace, I thought it might be a good time to go."

Richard surveyed his sister, but he couldn't read anything in her face as she stared out the window. He sank back in the seat and sighed. Whatever Susan was thinking, he had to remind himself that it had gotten him out of a miserable carriage ride with Lady Eleanor.

As the carriage pulled up to the Huxley townhouse, they were promptly met by the butler and directed to the drawing room. The townhouse was large and spacious, well decorated with royal blue and purple sashes, drapes, furniture upholstery and rugs, and rich red wooden furniture. He was familiar with the dining and ballrooms of the townhouse, but once they passed the grand hall, he felt lost. He remained in close proximity to his sister and the butler as they proceeded to the drawing room.

Miss Huxley was standing at the window, looking out over the grounds of her family's estate, unaware of their arrival. However, there was something that he noticed as they entered the room, something which made a strange hissing sound. Richard started, glancing around the room, anticipating something like a snake that had slipped in through an ajar door or a cracked window. But when the sound came again, it was clear it wasn't a snake. And he couldn't see from whence the sound was coming.

Chapter Five

Anne was deep in thought when she heard Mischief hiss. Without thinking, she followed him to the corner of the drawing room, to which he had retreated. She scooped him up, cradling him protectively as though he were an infant. He was happy to cling onto her, although his ears were pinned flat against his head and he was staring, wide-eyed, toward the door to the drawing room. Only then did Anne turn to see what it was that had disturbed him so. There stood Susan, her dearest friend, but Susan wasn't alone. Beside her was her brother, the duke of Calder. And he looked as unhappy as Mischief was acting.

Anne shook her head, giving her friend an openly irritated look, despite the expectations of propriety when welcoming guests. She could imagine her mother's cold eyes on her, and she didn't say a word right away, despite her mother's lacking presence. Susan gave her a sheepish look, shrugging ever so slightly. Meanwhile, the duke stood awkwardly at her side, giving Mischief a wary look.

Why would Susan bring her brother here unannounced? She wondered, her frustration mounting. It wasn't unusual for Susan herself to come without warning. But she had never taken it upon herself to invite someone along with her. Least of all, her brother.

After the embarrassment of the previous night, and the backlash she received from her mother about the scandal sheets, the last thing she was ready to tolerate was the presence of a duke who had always been enigmatic and daunting to her. She hardly knew if she could prepare herself to interact with him if she'd been given advance warning, let alone when his arrival came as a complete surprise.

Mischief gave a low growl, snapping Anne back to the present moment. She forced herself to curtsey, although the displeasure never left her expression.

"Susan," Anne said pointedly, glaring at her friend once more. Then, she glanced briefly at the duke, who was now looking at her with unreadable blue eyes. "Your Grace. What a surprise."

Susan gave Anne a timid smile, her eyes filled with an apology that Anne wasn't quite ready to accept.

"I do hope we're not intruding," she said. "We thought we'd stop by for a brief visit."

Anne opened her mouth, but she quickly bit her tongue. Even though her mother wasn't there, she imagined that the viscountess's eyes would be narrowed at her, waiting for her to say or do something untoward. Whilst she was longing to do so, she was aware that she was already in dire straits for the chaos she had wrought the eve prior. It wouldn't do to say or do something that the duke might report back to her mother.

"Please, come in," she said, albeit through clenched teeth. She managed another curtsey, despite her simmering irritation. What in the world was the duke doing in her home? They had never spoken more than a few obligatory words to one another at social events, particularly when she was chatting with Susan, and he happened to be nearby. She couldn't imagine what would make him wish to accompany his sister to Anne's family's home, especially without a specific reason.

Mischief, who had finally straightened his ears and relaxed his body, nestled sweetly against her chest. She shifted her arms to hold the animal more securely, idly kissing him atop his ginger head and feeling a vibrating sensation against her bosom as he began purring.

Anne unbiddenly recalled how her mother had pointedly left her out of the shopping trip on which Charlotte and she had embarked. It seemed like a continuation of the reprimand she received from the viscountess that morning, and it pained her greatly. She knew she had embarrassed her family, even though she felt they were treating her unfairly by not hearing her side of the story. But was her mother so ashamed of her now that she wouldn't be seen in public with her?

As Susan and the Duke of Calder settled into their seats, one of the servants poured them tea and served them cakes. Susan dutifully accepted hers, while the duke merely gave a stern nod, his eyes never leaving Anne and Mischief. Anne wondered if he had an aversion to felines, and she considered finding out by taking the cat to him and offering to let him pet the animal.

She could feel a small smile play on her lips at the thought of Mischief batting his hand away with another hiss. In her arms, she knew that the cat would feel safe and unthreatened, and he would let the duke know precisely what his mistress and he thought about his arrival.

Before she could do anything, Susan cleared her throat, glancing nervously at Anne.

"How are you faring this morning, Anne?" she asked, once more giving Anne an apologetic look.

Anne opened her mouth, wanting to point out that if Susan rushed over in such a hurry, she must know perfectly well how Anne was faring. But with the duke present, she knew she couldn't say anything improper or distasteful. Besides, she didn't want to discuss such troubles in front of a man whom she hardly knew and who made her feel so completely ill at ease with his imposing demeanor.

"I'm still a bit surprised by your visit," she said, glancing pointedly at Richard.

The duke cleared his throat, adjusting the bow tie around his neck. He didn't say anything, but he raised his eyebrow at Anne. If Anne didn't know better, he seemed to be daring her to point out his presence. It was all she could do to not do that as she looked at her friend again.

Susan nodded, trying to force a bright smile.

"It has been ages since I came to visit, my dearest," she said brightly. "I was hoping that, perhaps, we could go to Gunter's for ices. I brought Richard along so that we would have an escort."

Anne felt another surge of surprise, one which seemed to travel across the room and register on the duke's face. Clearly, he hadn't been let in on his sister's plan ahead of time, which made Anne all the more curious. Why would Susan bring her brother without telling him why? Susan had never been one for craftiness or keeping secrets.

She recalled the letter she had sent to her friend, figuring that must have been what brought Susan unannounced. But it still didn't explain why she would plan a sudden trip to Gunter's and bring her brother as a chaperone. Anne was becoming more puzzled by the minute, and she was struggling to not bluntly ask her friend what was going on.

She cast her eyes upon the duke, who beheld his sister with equal bewilderment, mirroring the perplexity Anne herself experienced.

She waited for him to protest, thinking that he would have better things to do than to escort his younger sister and her friend whom he hardly knew to get ice treats. Instead, however, he nodded silently in agreement. His gaze was fixed firmly on Susan, but she seemed relieved that he had agreed. It was as if she had been counting on her brother to agree to her plan. Once more, Anne wondered what her friend had in mind.

As she watched the silent interaction between the siblings, the duke gave her a contemplative glance. She looked away quickly, pretending to be looking for something. She wasn't usually shy about speaking what was on her mind. But she didn't want to offend a duke, even if he was the brother of her best friend. Perhaps, especially the brother of her dearest friend. And yet the whole situation began to bother her the more she thought it over. Nothing made any sense, and she earnestly desired to openly inquire of Susan what her intentions were.

As she was pretending to look around the room for something she wouldn't be able to describe if either of her guests asked if they could help her, she cast a sideways look at the duke once more. He was still silent, but he was giving his sister an inquisitive look. Susan shrugged, also remaining silent, and the discomfort welling up in Anne was about to overflow. She took a deep, slow breath, trying to think of something to say to break the silence. As she did so, she noticed the duke looking at her with that same odd look.

I might faint from anticipation, she thought, turning herself toward her friend and Richard. She wasn't sure what she was going to say. But she was sure that if she didn't say something, the tension in the room would send her into a state of madness.

"When would the two of you like to go?" she asked, her voice exceedingly strained to the extent that it caused her great distress.

Susan looked at her with sympathy, her eyes apologetic, but for what, Anne couldn't guess.

"Any time you're ready, my dearest," she said, giving Anne a reassuring smile. "Pray, proceed at your leisure. We are in no undue haste."

The Duke turned his head to look at his sister as though to object. But he seemed to think better of it, giving Anne a quick glance and a curt nod.

"Any time you like," he murmured.

Anne nodded, her heart suddenly pounding. He looked very unhappy about the situation, whatever that situation might truly be. But she couldn't help noticing how beautiful his blue eyes were. She shook her head, idly stroking Mischief, who had begun to stir in her arms. She realized that if she wanted answers, or if she wanted to get the day over with, she would need to be ready to leave soon.

Before she could voice her decision to leave right then, Mischief wriggled from her arms, jumping down onto the table that separated her from Susan and the duke. He shook himself, stretching slowly before sauntering over to the duke and plopping himself down right in front of him. Anne's eyes widened in fear, wondering what her cat was about to do. She thought it was adorable when he swatted at her clothing. But she didn't think that the Duke would be too amused if the feline did it to his coat.

Anne gave Susan a look, but she looked as though she was concerned. The standoff between the animal and the duke gave a much needed reprieve from the tension, but Anne couldn't help being nervous, not knowing how Mischief would react to the Duke, or how the duke would react to the cat. Susan rose from her seat, watching her brother carefully as Mischief flicked his tail and stared up at the duke. Anne held her breath, unsure of what might happen. But once again, the duke surprised her. He held out his hand, allowing Mischief to sniff it.

"He's really a darling cat," Susan said, reaching out gently to scratch him behind the ears.

Mischief pulled back, not because of Susan, but because there was a new person in the room. He had always been a bit standoffish around people when he first saw them, which Anne attributed to his abandonment when he was a kitten. The duke didn't seem fazed, however. He gave the cat a small smirk before turning to Anne.

"Are you ready?" he asked.

Anne looked at Mischief, who looked ready to do precisely what she feared. She nodded, realizing that there was something she would need before they departed. She hurried over to Mischief, picking him up and scratching him gently as she placed him across the room from her guests, on the soft cushion in front of the large window that overlooked the front lawn of her family's townhouse. Mischief mewed in complaint, glancing behind her at the duke as though wanting to finish the confrontation. But at last, he sniffed, kneading the cushion with his front paws before curling up into a ball and lying in the warm sunshine.

Anne sighed with relief, moving to the coat rack by the door of the drawing room, where one of her pelisses hung.

"Yes, I am ready," she said, offering the duke a sheepish smile. "I apologise for Mischief. It takes him some time to get accustomed to new people."

Richard shrugged, glancing over to where the cat now lay sleeping.

"No harm done, Miss Huxley," he said.

Anne nodded, reaching for her pelisse. She glanced at Susan, who was straightening her own coat and smoothing out her skirt. What might be Susan's intent as she precipitously appeared in the company of her brother and exhibits peculiar conduct? What could a person who was not known for scheming be planning?

Chapter Six

Richard remained silent during his sister's interaction with Miss Anne Huxley, but his suspicion was aroused. He had believed that his sister meant to save him from their tyrannical mother earlier that morning. But now that she had unveiled a desire to go into town and use him as an escort, he was beginning to sense an ulterior motive for his sister's sudden desire to drag him to Miss Huxley's house. He was aware that Susan was close friends with her, and he was accustomed to seeing her at different gatherings. However, he had never spoken more than a few words to her when it was socially required of him to do so.

In the beginning, the part of him that perpetually anticipated his mother's endeavours to find him a suitable match, entertained the notion that Susan and Miss Huxley might be conspiring to unite him with Miss Huxley. However, the evident surprise and irritation on the young lady's face when they arrived had immediately erased any such suspicion. On the other hand, he still hadn't discounted the fact that his sister might be secretly planning such a match. He might have thought their mother put Susan up to such deceit. But his mother's adamant revulsion over Miss Huxley's appearance in the scandal sheets ruled that out completely as a possibility.

What could Susan be up to? He wondered, giving his sister a pointed look as they settled into the carriage. Miss Huxley and her lady's maid were trailing behind, whispering amongst themselves. He could hardly voice his fears or displeasure with Miss Huxley nearby. But he knew Susan would understand with a simple look that she was treading on thin ice.

If she was up to some sort of matchmaking scheme, he would not tolerate it. He wanted to give her the benefit of the doubt because he loved his younger sister. But he couldn't help being wary, especially with the sheepish expression on her face. He raised an eyebrow, giving Susan a subtle shake of his head. If she noticed it, she didn't acknowledge it. Instead, she leaned closer to him, dropping her voice low.

"Brother," she said, looking at him with eyes that pleaded for understanding. "I have an idea, and I know it will sound completely mad. Will you hear it?"

Richard sighed. He knew then that his suspicions were correct. He didn't know if he wanted to hear his sister's plan, but he felt he had little choice. And he had even less time before Miss Huxley and her lady's maid joined them in the coach.

"Very well," he said with another sigh. "Tell me what it is that you're scheming."

Susan gave him a small smile, glancing out the window to see where her friend was.

"What if we could put an end to Mother's relentless matchmaking once and for all?" she asked.

Richard frowned, looking at his sister even more cautiously.

"If your brilliant idea is to match me with Miss Huxley, you must be forgetting exactly how supportive Mother would be of that notion," he hissed.

Susan grimaced at Richard's sharp tone. Guilt filled Richard and he sighed once more.

"Forgive me, Sister," he said with resignation. "I am simply weary of the discourse surrounding my prospective marriage. Pray, proceed."

Susan nodded, though her expression was notably calmer and more guarded.

"Anne's parents have been pressing her to accept the advances that her cousin, Albert Harrow, is making toward her," she whispered. "And I understand that they are making plans to force her into marrying him. They are quite displeased about what the scandal sheets say about her."

Richard nodded curtly, unable to hide his distaste for the man. He knew that Lord Harrow was a heavy drinker, had been known to lose large sums of money to gambling, and it was whispered that he had been in the company of numerous ladies. Even at his age, Richard understood that he behaved like a young rogue, and yet he seemed to manage to hold some prestige to his name due to his familial ties to the viscount and viscountess Huxley. Even though he didn't know Miss Huxley very well, he felt a pang of sympathy at her plight.

"Pray, allow me to conjecture," Richard said, keeping his voice low. "Your proposal entails arranging a connection between Miss Huxley and myself, thus enabling us to evade the lamentable shackles of unions with individuals whom we abhor?" Ordinarily, that would have been a implausible guess. But considering the way his sister had suddenly saved him from that horrible tea with Lady Eleanor and her mother, her sudden decision to drop in on Miss Huxley, and now, her telling him about Miss Huxley's plight, it made perfect sense to Richard. And the expression on Susan's face confirmed Richard's hypothesis.

"It's worth considering, is it not?" she asked.

Richard shook his head, even though the thought was taking root in his mind already.

"It would be utterly impracticable to achieve such a feat," he said. "Besides, what makes you think that Miss Huxley would ever agree to such a wild idea?"

Susan shrugged.

"I believe she would do anything to avoid marrying her cousin," she said.

Richard chuckled softly.

"What a reason to marry a gentleman," he said dryly.

Susan reached out and put her hand over his.

"I don't mean to imply that you are not a worthy husband," she said. "But the two of you do not have much time. Something must be done quickly to prevent the two of you from ending up in miserable marriages. And Anne isn't one of those shallow, arrogant ton ladies, like Lady Eleanor and her friends."

Richard shook his head again, but deep down, he was thinking over his sister's suggestion.

"How do you propose we accomplish a wedding?" he asked. "No one would ever believe that we suddenly decided that we wanted to marry each other. Especially not Mother." *And we both know that Mother is hardly a fan of Miss Huxley, and would never approve of such a match,* he added silently, not daring to speak the words aloud with Miss Huxley so close.

Susan chewed her lip, noticing how close her friend was to the carriage. She looked at Richard, her eyes filled with urgency, clearly determined to finish explaining her plan before Miss Huxley boarded the coach.

"What if we were to stage a courtship between Anne and you?" she asked. "It would show Mother that you are at least giving a search for a bride a real try, and perhaps keep her from pushing any more young ladies on you. It would keep Anne from being forced into marrying her cousin, at least until her parents gave up on the idea. And once everyone was properly convinced, the two of you could call off your courtship. Or not, if you chose to marry to ensure that you never had to face the chance of marrying someone you dislike in the future."

Richard shook his head, even though he couldn't bring himself to protest. It was a crazy idea, to be sure, especially if they were only faking a courtship. It would eventually end, as they would only be doing it to fool their respective families. That could lead to scandal, particularly for Miss Huxley. And Richard thought she had likely had more than enough time in the scandal sheets, especially since she was not a compromised woman.

And yet, there was an appeal to his sister's plan. Such a pretend courtship would, indeed, protect both of them from their family's interjections into their lives. And clearly, Miss Huxley was, as Susan had said, not one of the snobby, gossiping women whom Richard despised. She might have made a name for herself as a woman who acted out at gatherings. But she was also not afraid to say what she was thinking, even if it jeopardized her reputation within the ton. That was something Richard could respect. At least, his time spent with her wouldn't feel oppressive and miserable.

But before he could voice his reservations or consent, Miss Huxley and her maid were assisted into the carriage by a footman. Anne's presence disrupted the conversation, and Richard was left to stew in his thoughts as they set off on their journey to Gunter's.

The atmosphere inside the carriage was just as tense as it had been in the drawing room of the Huxley townhouse. Richard didn't mind the silence, as his mind was filled with thoughts of his sister's idea. In any other circumstance, he would have surmised that she had been ensnared by his mother's aspirations for him to enter into matrimony. But he knew that she loved Miss Huxley deeply and she seemed to genuinely want to help Richard avoid entering a marriage that would make him miserable for the rest of his life.

However, he couldn't fathom how they would ever get their mother over such a notion. He knew there was likely never any chance that the dowager duchess would ever accept Miss Huxley as a viable marriage option for him. But nor did he think she would be any more agreeable to him ending the courtship when they felt sure they had escaped meddling families trying to arrange marriages for them. He couldn't help smiling to himself. In truth, he didn't care if his mother approved. As far as he was concerned, it would befit her justly for pushing women he didn't want onto him. Why couldn't he have his turn to push a woman that she didn't like onto her?

Normally, the ride to Gunter's would have only taken about half an hour. But with the silence in the carriage, it seemed to be taking much longer. Richard had pulled himself back to the present moment and into the lingering silence. He thought it was odd that a woman who was normally not afraid to say anything hadn't spoken more than a few words, especially considering how close she and Susan were. He supposed she might be as shocked and suspicious of Susan as he had been. He thought it was interesting that, if that were the case, they thought so much alike when they hardly knew each other.

Just when Richard thought the tension might swallow them all, Susan perked up. She smiled brightly at Miss Huxley, who looked at Susan warily.

"What flavours of ices should we get?" she asked.

Miss Huxley looked just as surprised at the sudden casual conversation topic as she had been when Richard and Susan had arrived at her home. She stared at Susan, and for a moment, Richard thought she would finally ask what Susan was up to. Instead, however, she shrugged, opening her mouth and closing it a couple of times before she finally answered.

"Strawberry," she said. "I like the strawberry ones."

Richard nodded, keeping silent. The strawberry ices were his favorite, but he was content to let the two women talk.

"I would like a rhubarb one," Susan said, sighing happily. "Raspberry is my favourite, but I understand that those might not be available until later this summer."

Miss Huxley seemed to relax, if only a little. She nodded, giving Susan a small smile.

"I enjoy a raspberry sorbet," she said. "Perhaps, you and I could go and get one of those once raspberries are in season."

Richard picked up on the emphasis when Miss Huxley said 'you and I.' He took no offense, however. He knew she must have been stunned to have him just show up at her home.

Susan nodded, her smile full of relief, now that her friend was speaking to her.

"That would be delightful," she said.

As the two women continued discussing the iced cakes and the ice cream flavors served during the summer and autumn at Gunter's, Richard sneaked looks at his sister's friend. Now that he had the chance to really look at her, he was surprised to notice that she was quite beautiful. Her jade green eyes, which were slowly losing their suspicious glint, sparkled as she laughed at something Susan said to her. Her auburn hair was pinned loosely atop her head with diamond combs, framing her porcelain face perfectly.

Perhaps, Susan and Thomas are onto something, he thought, allowing himself to picture how it would look to engage in a pretend courtship with Miss Huxley. She might find her way into the scandal sheets from time to time. But there was nothing she had done that Richard found even remotely repulsive or distasteful. As he listened, he noticed how musical her laugh was, and how sweet and light her voice was when she spoke. Now that she had relaxed, she seemed to be enjoying herself. He could certainly do worse than Miss Huxley, that much was true. But what would she think of such an arrangement? What if Susan was wrong, and she wouldn't agree to such a sham?

As the carriage pulled up to Gunter's, Richard's mind was still a whirl of thoughts and ideas. He shook off the notion for the moment, focusing on the afternoon ahead. He assisted Susan out of the carriage, and then, he offered his hand to her friend. The brief contact of their fingers sent an unexpected warmth coursing

52

through his arm, and he had to force himself to withdraw his hand slowly, so as to not appear to be recoiling from her in disgust.

The sensation was fleeting, yet potent. A mixture of feelings he couldn't quite identify lingered within him as they stepped into Gunter's. He still wasn't sure if he would agree with his sister's plan. But he couldn't deny that the more he thought about it, and the more he looked at Miss Huxley, the more intriguing it sounded.

Chapter Seven

The tension of the carriage ride to Gunter's dissolved the instant Anne's hand touched that of the Duke of Calder. For a single instant, all she was aware of was just how handsome he was, with his black, unruly hair peeking out from beneath his hat and his shrewd blue eyes with, until that brief moment, always appeared hard and disinterested. It had made her heart race, and the moment seemed as though it lasted forever. But the second that the world came back into focus around Anne as they stepped inside Gunter's, it was as if the strange, tingly moment had never occurred.

She had been too nervous on the ride into town to think about anything except the disrupting sudden arrival of Susan and the duke at her home and the unplanned outing to the tea-house. But as conversations ceased abruptly and scrutinizing, judgmental eyes shifted straight to Anne's face as they made their way to a table, it occurred to her why she should have reconsidered showing her face in public the same day that her most recent feat made its way to the scandal sheets.

She pointed her gaze to the floor, but the damage was already done. She could hear people whispering as she and her little group walked past, and her cheeks were growing noticeably redder by the second. It was bad enough that the other patrons of the tea-house were judging her. But as they passed one particularly large table, she heard someone whispering about Susan and the duke. They could very well be ostracized for being affiliated with her. She couldn't bear to bring shame on people who didn't deserve it.

To her surprise, however, the duke stayed right by her side. He cunningly linked his arm through hers and stood up perfectly straight with his head held high. He glanced around the room with his typical stern expression, which sent many clusters of people turning quickly away from their group and taking their eyes off Anne. She understood that he was likely using his imposing status to protect himself and his sister. Nonetheless, she was grateful for the reprieve it granted her from at least a few of the other customers.

As they took their seats in a corner table in the tea-house, Richard silently excused himself to order their ice treats. Anne saw her opportunity and couldn't keep her questions in any longer. She put her lips to her friend's ear and prayed that the duke would remain occupied by speaking to the waitress long enough for her to interrogate her friend.

"What is the meaning of all this?" she hissed, looking at Susan as though she had gone mad. "You come to my home with your brother without announcement, and then you drag me here. Surely, you saw the scandal sheets. I am delighted to see you, but I wonder what your motives could possibly be."

Susan looked at Anne with eyes that seemed a bit too wide and innocent.

"I got the note you sent to me," she said. "One of your footmen brought it to me this morning. And as far as me bringing Richard with me, he needed an escape from our mother. Nothing more."

Anne nodded, disbelieving more than half of what her friend said. Susan was typically very straightforward with her. But there was something in her eyes that made Anne acutely suspicious. It was possible that one of the footmen had delivered her letter to Susan. It wouldn't be the first time, and she was grateful that her friend knew what was troubling her. But if that was the case, it made it that much more baffling as to why Susan would bring the duke along with her. How did Susan expect her to speak about something so personal with a man, who was basically a stranger to her, present?

To Anne's chagrin, their hushed conversation didn't go unnoticed by the nearby patrons, and curious glances were cast their way. Anne fought the urge to bury her face in her hands as she had that morning and try to pretend that she wasn't there. Why had she ever agreed to leave the safety and peace of her home with Susan and the Duke of Calder?

"Susan," she whispered frantically, purposely avoiding the gazes of even the closest patrons. "Do you really think this was a good idea?"

55

Susan gazed upon Anne, clearly devoid of any comprehension of the whispered commotion encircling them. Anne glanced around pointedly, which guided Susan's eyes to the groups of people who were clearly trying to listen in on their conversations. As soon as the realization hit her, Susan blushed, and she opened her mouth to speak. But just then, the duke returned with three ice treats in his hands. Anne glowered at her friend, promptly sitting up straight and pretending to ignore the stares of the people around them, just as she pretended that her cheeks weren't flaming red.

Just as he had when they had entered the tea-house, the duke glanced around at the tables nearest to them with a stern, no-nonsense expression on his face. Anne blushed, realizing that he must have heard some of the whispers, and she felt terrible that he had to protect her, even in such a covert manner.

As he took his seat, which happened to be beside her, Anne opened her mouth to apologize and ask if they should just leave. But as he placed her fruit ice in front of her, she realized, to her surprise, that he was still holding a strawberry treat. Not only must he have been paying attention when she was talking about the fruit ices with Susan in the carriage but it seemed as though they had the same opinions about them.

"It seems we have similar tastes in ices, Your Grace," she said with a soft giggle.

To her surprise, the duke gave her a warm smile, raising his fruit ice to her in a gesture of a toast.

"Strawberry ices are the best ones here, in my humble opinion," he said.

Susan, always quick with a witty remark, grinned at the two of them.

"Oh, Brother," she said. "I believe that makes the two of you intellectual equals, at least in matters of frozen treats."

Richard smirked, his eyes glinting mischievously.

"Great minds think alike, I suppose," he said.

Anne studied the duke carefully. If she didn't know better, she might have thought he was flirting with her. But she knew that was impossible. No one of his station would ever consider a romance with her, especially not after her appearance in that day's

56

scandal sheets. She reminded herself that he was simply trying to protect her from the prying eyes and the hateful whispers of the other patrons. She couldn't deny that she was glad for his commitment to shielding her, even if it were only for propriety's sake.

With that, the ice was broken, both in the sense of the easing of the tension that had clung to everyone since Susan and the duke had arrived at Anne's home, and in the fact that they each enjoyed their ices. She was still uncertain as to what had made Susan make such a spontaneous trip. But once she got the taste of her strawberry fruit ice on her tongue, she was glad that her friend had acted so impulsively.

When the duke snorted, she glanced over at Susan and saw that she had rhubarb juice dribbling down her chin. She could help giggling, which caused some of her own juice to trickle over her lip. These circumstances provoked Anne to laugh even harder, and before long, both Susan and she were struggling to contain their mirth.

The duke laughed, pulling out two handkerchiefs, handing one to Susan. Then, he handed one to Anne, his eyes sparkling with warm amusement.

"That would make a lovely shade of lipstick, I believe," he said with a small wink.

Anne's heard skipped as she took the handkerchief, feeling her cheeks turn as red as her fruit ice.

"Perhaps, we should submit that to the department stores nearby," she said, pointing to Susan. "That would be a lovely shade, as well."

Susan pretended to glower at Anne, but she was still smiling broadly. She dabbed at her mouth, the pink juice leaving a mouth-shaped stain on her brother's handkerchief. Anne pulled hers away from her face and saw that hers looked much the same, only with a deeper red color. She laughed again, grateful for the lighthearted fun. And the duke was surprising her with his warm and carefree disposition. She had only seen him as firm and aloof. It was a pleasant surprise to see that he could enjoy a little silliness, even in public, as well.

Their jovial conversation, however, was abruptly halted by the arrival of Lady Beatrice, Lord Gray's cousin who was notorious for being one of the biggest gossips in all of London. The tall, rail-thin, raven-haired woman approached, looking down her nose at the trio sitting at their table, with the four women who followed her everywhere right on the tail of her purple dress.

Anne felt a pang of unease under Beatrice's predatory gaze. She discreetly sipped her drink, her hand trembling as Susan attempted to divert the women's attention.

"Richard," she said, beaming a little too sweetly at her brother. "Didn't you say that you would take us shopping after this?"

The duke didn't miss a beat once he took a look at Anne's face. He grinned broadly, giving her another small wink, invisible to Lady Beatrice and her entourage.

"I certainly did," he said. "And if we are still out around supper time, we shall find a nice place to eat before we return home."

Anne offered him a weak smile, but she couldn't shake the sensation of five sets of eyes fixed directly on her. She tried to appear unfazed, but her whole body was starting to tremble. It was bad enough that the entire tea-house had been whispering about her earlier. What would happen now that Lady Beatrice had spotted her sitting with the duke of Calder?

Lady Beatrice was undeterred by being so blatantly ignored. With a honey smile, she dipped into a mocking curtsey.

"Your Grace, how odd to see you in such," she paused, giving Anne a long, cold, hateful look up and down, "unusual company."

The veiled insult was not lost on Anne. She steadied herself, preparing for what was to come. She had thought that, once the other patrons had gone back to minding their business, there would be no trouble or embarrassment for Susan or her brother. But she had clearly been very wrong, and she felt both mortified and ashamed. She should have never agreed to go out into public with them. And now, they would suffer gossip spreading about them, just as it did about her.

She sat up straight, determined to hold her head high and pretend that she was unbothered by Lady Beatrice. But when she tried to speak, she found that her voice failed her. This caused the women surrounding Lady Beatrice to titter with giggles, and Lady Beatrice herself gave Anne a cold, evil smirk. She swallowed, taking another sip of her melting fruit ice. *Please, do not let me say or do something that will make this situation any worse than it already is,* she prayed silently to the heavens.

As she floundered for a response to the cruel women who were still boring holes through Anne with their burning gazes, the Duke rose, straightening his coat and looking Lady Beatrice right in the eyes.

"Miss Huxley is my sister's dear friend," he said. "I hardly see why it's any of your business with whom I spend my time."

Anne stared at the duke, surprised that he was still stepping in to help her. Lady Beatrice, however, was completely unmoved. She batted her eyelashes, glancing at Susan with a look that bordered somewhere between disgust and pity.

"What a shame," she said, blinking rapidly at the duke. "I always rather liked Susan. It's a pity that she associates herself with someone as troublesome as her."

Anne's embarrassment began to transition to the same anger she had felt the night before when Lord Gray had issued his snide remarks. What gave anyone the right to be so judgmental, especially when they had been sitting there, minding their own business? And who was Lady Beatrice to think she could attack someone as sweet and innocent as Susan? It was becoming harder for her to keep her wits about her, even though she was with a duke. She didn't take kindly to people being nasty to her loved once, and Lady Beatrice knew very well that Anne would react if she persisted.

"Lady Beatrice," Richard said, putting a toxic emphasis on her name as he addressed the hateful woman. "I am with the exact manner of company that I happen to prefer. Their refreshing perspectives are far more stimulating and intriguing than that of the usual drab, boring society banter. There is nothing more dull or tasteless than gossip, talk of dress shopping and feigning interest in musical instruments to try to prove how special people are."

Lady Beatrice's face fell instantly, her cheeks growing first pink, then red, then crimson, almost to the point of purple as she cycled through various shades of embarrassment. She looked around at the women behind her, who kept their eyes to the floor. It seemed that, as foolish and empty-headed as they were, they had sense enough to look chastised when scolded by a duke.

She took a deep breath, straightening her shoulders. Her eyes never left those of the duke, but she looked wounded and sulking.

"Good day to you," she said curtly, turning on her heel. In her flustered state, she bumped into the woman who was closest to her. She shoved her shoulder into the woman, pushing her aside. Then, the women marched away, leaving Anne swimming in a sea of emotions.

She glanced at the Duke, expecting to see that his aloof coldness had returned. She could hardly blame him, after all, especially after such an embarrassing encounter. But to her utter shock, he was looking right at her, and when their eyes met, he gave her a playful smirk.

"I think we can finish our ices and leave as soon as you are ready, Miss Huxley," he said.

Anne blushed again, this time from the sparkle in the duke's eyes. But she nodded, giving him a grateful smile.

"Thank you," she mouthed, putting a cold hand to her burning cheek.

The duke shrugged, smiling once more.

"My pleasure," he mouthed in return.

As they finished their ices and prepared to depart, the duke rose first. He offered his arm to Anne, his eyes still warm and reassuring. She took it timidly, her cheeks heating once more. She glanced at Susan, who looked like she could burst with excitement. Still reeling from all the events of the afternoon, she allowed the duke to lead her out of Gunter's.

When they emerged onto the bustling street, Anne couldn't help but contemplate the confining standards which society imposed on women. She hadn't done anything that warranted society to shun her so, and, yet, she was being treated just as though she had soiled her reputation in other ways. She also considered the ease with which the duke had dismissed the gossiping women.

60

She marveled that a man of his refined nature and status would get involved. But more than that, it had seemed to come from a place of genuine protectiveness. Was it just because she was his sister's best friend? Gratitude, confusion, and a growing curiosity about the enigmatic duke of Calder swirled within Anne's mind. She still didn't know why Susan had brought him with her that day. But she was starting to be very glad that she had.

Chapter Eight

"Richard," the dowager duchess said as Richard passed his mother's pink parlor after returning with Susan. "Where have you been? It's nearly time to prepare for dinner."

Richard reluctantly paused outside the door, carefully peeking inside to see if she still had her guests. The room was blissfully empty apart from his mother, however, and he allowed himself to relax just a little.

"Susan asked me to serve as her escort in town after our first stop," he said truthfully. There was no reason to mention with whom his sister and he had spent the early afternoon. Lady Beatrice had tried to disrupt their outing with her nonsense, but Richard had succeeded in embarrassing her enough that he felt sure she would make no mention of it to anyone who wasn't present.

The dowager eyed him suspiciously, and he knew what was coming.

"I wonder why Susan would make no mention of any such trips to town before today," she said curtly. "Especially when she knew there were guests arriving who expected to see you."

Richard shrugged. He had told Susan to go to her chambers when they returned home so that their mother would not be too hard on her. As her older brother, he felt very protective of her. And besides, he had ended up enjoying the hours he spent with his sister and Miss Huxley that day.

"I imagine that, with all the other hype with my marriage paring and the guests arriving, Susan might have easily forgotten," he said. "And surely, you would not wish for Susan to leave home without a proper escort."

At this, the duchess blanched. His mother was very prim and proper, and the thought of her only daughter being improperly escorted in town would be abhorrent to her.

It turned out that he was correct. His mother shuddered, her face relaxing into a softer, less angry expression.

"You are a good brother," she said, sounding both proud and resigned. "However, you and your sister must inform me of such outings before I embarrass myself, as I did with Eleanor and her mother today."

Richard gave his mother an indulgent smile and bowed.

"Of course, Mother," he said. "I shall speak with Susan and remind her of this. Thank you for your understanding."

The dowager sniffed, then returned to her knitting. Richard took that as his cue to escape, hurrying to his private study. He didn't need to work that day, but he knew it would be best if he looked busy. He didn't want his mother to get the idea that he had time to make up the missed tea encounter with Lady Eleanor and her mother that day.

He was sure that the dowager would have invited them to dinner soon, and that was painful enough for him. He couldn't allow his mother to try to squeeze in any extra time for the forward Lady Eleanor to intrude on his life. He pulled out a fresh ledger book and began filling in details he would need for the following month. He had no data to put in them, but he knew he could drag out the task of preparing the pages for the data that would come at the beginning of the following month. Anything was better than further conversation with his mother, and certainly, entertaining Lady Eleanor for even five minutes.

Late that evening, when Richard was bored to tears with pretending to have important work to do, he poured himself a tumbler half full of brandy and sank back in his chair. He was surrounded by the portraits of many of his ancestors, past dukes, their wives and their sons, who in turn took over the dukedom. The room was filled with a feeling of nostalgia, and the flickering candlelight cast shadows across their stern, painted faces. He sipped his brandy, his mind drifting from the day in which his portrait would join that of his father on that same wall, to the afternoon's events.

It had been an eventful day, and all the memories remained clear and vivid. He had arrived at Miss Huxley's home with great reluctance, wondering if he hadn't made a mistake by allowing his sister to drag him there as opposed to staying and suffering through tea with Lady Eleanor. And when she had unveiled her wild idea that he should pretend to court Miss Huxley, he had been torn between thinking that his sister was utterly brilliant and completely crazy.

And when the cat approached him, Richard had been expecting to find himself bitten or scratched. But the animal had just sat there, staring at him as though trying to gaze into his soul. He smiled softly to himself as he thought about the animal's orange eyes. Richard himself didn't have any pets, but he had to admit that the cat was a little bit cute.

However, once he started paying attention to his sister's friend, he noticed how pretty and sweet she was. She was clearly smart and clever, and she had been excellent company at Gunter's. She was also good at holding her head high, even with all the whispers and stares as their little group sat enjoying their treats. It had been clear that it bothered her, and for a moment, Richard had thought she might make one of her scenes to try to stop everyone's gossiping. He could hardly have blamed her, as it was detestable the way people were behaving. But she handled herself well, and Richard had been impressed.

He had surprised himself by defending her as adamantly as he had when Lady Beatrice had approached, clearly looking to goad Miss Huxley into one of her stunts. Richard thought back to the ball, which had earned Miss Huxley her most recent mention in the scandal sheets. She was famous within the ton for doing things similar to what she had done to Lord Gray, as well as having clumsy accidents that were embarrassing, but hardly dangerous. He couldn't help wondering now how many of those incidents had been induced by people goading her, just as Lady Beatrice had tried to do. It put her in a different light to Richard, and he felt a pang of sympathy.

The distant chime of a dinner bell disrupted his thoughts, and he sighed deeply, reluctantly tearing his gaze away from the portraits. He knew he had to prepare for the impending evening. His mother had surely not forgotten that he had abandoned their guests at teatime. And he was sure she would not let him leave the dinner table without giving him an earful about it. Reluctantly, Richard dragged himself from his chair, stretching the muscles in his back that had gone stiff from his hours of pretending to be busy. Then, he slowly made his way through the halls, unhappily heading for the dining room.

As he anticipated, his mother met his gaze the instant he entered the room with her own steely one. Susan was yet to arrive for dinner, so it was just his mother and him. The dowager waited for him to take his seat before she spoke.

"I trust that you will not be busy the next time I invite Eleanor and Victoria to visit," she said, her voice clipped and intense.

Richard shrugged, holding his mother's gaze.

"You will need to let me know in advance next time," he said. "You know I am away a great deal on business, and I will always escort Susan into town when she wants to go. She is my younger sister, and she needs my protection."

His mother sniffed, clearly not as moved by the sentiment as she had been earlier that day.

"Susan can take her lady's maid," she said. "You have other duties to fulfill. Those include helping me entertain guests. Especially when they come primarily to see you."

Richard shrugged again, at last tearing his eyes away from his mother and looking at his bowl, which was being filled with soup.

"I will try to keep open space in my schedule," he lied, taking a spoonful of the steaming broth. "But I must know enough in advance."

His mother eyed him warily, clearly wanting to say something more. But just then, Susan entered, so she dropped the subject.

"Did you enjoy your trip to town, Daughter?" the dowager asked, clearly engaging in a quest for additional enlightenment than what Richard had given her.

Susan must have been prepared, because she beamed at her mother.

"It was lovely, Mother," she said. "I asked the library to reserve a couple of books for me when next they are returned. Then, we went to have fruit ices at Gunter's, and we took a little stroll along Bond Street."

The dowager nodded, studying her daughter suspiciously. In the end, however, she must have decided that Susan was telling the truth. She merely sighed, helping herself to some of her own soup.

"Please be sure to remind me when you are taking trips like that," she said. "I looked rather foolish today when the two of you ran off while we had guests."

Susan gave her mother a sheepish smile, shooting Richard a look with a sparkle in her eyes.

"I apologise, Mother," she said. "I will ensure that you are aware from now on."

The dowager nodded, and they ate their soup in silence. As the second course of the meal was served, however, the duchess spoke again.

"We must never forget the importance of propriety," she said, sounding as though she was hinting at something. "We have a duty to our peers in the ton to be examples of what upstanding nobility should be."

Richard nodded, but he wanted to roll his eyes. His mother's strict sense of propriety had stifled him all his life. But lately, it had been far worse. And he knew that was because she so desperately wanted him to marry.

"Of course, Mother," Susan said, once more saving her brother. "We will always uphold the highest standards of propriety."

It was all Richard could do to not choke on his wine as his sister spoke. He heard the irony in his sister's words, and he knew that she was thinking about that afternoon, as well. He thought again about her proposal to pretend to court Miss Huxley. *The highest standards, indeed,* he thought, wrestling to hold back his laughter.

The duchess didn't seem to notice, however. She simply huffed a little, sipping her own wine before turning her gaze back to Richard.

"Richard, dear, you know how vital it is to consider the future of the Calder legacy," she said. "A lady like Eleanor would be the perfect duchess, don't you think?"

Richard forced himself to keep a straight face, though the notion horrified him. That was the very reason he had even given Susan's suggestion a second thought. He could never bring himself to marry a woman like Lady Eleanor. And he had no intention of giving his mother the impression that he would even consider it.

"It's been a long day, Mother," he said. "We can finish this conversation another time."

The dowager glowered at her son, clearly displeased. But she said nothing further, and they finished their dinner in peace.

After the strained meal, Richard slipped away unnoticed, heading straight for Thomas's townhouse. Thomas, who had just finished dinner himself, invited him in warmly, guiding him straight to the comforting familiarity of his billiard room. He poured them both a glass of port, fetching them both a cigar. Richard took both from Thomas, giving him a grateful smile.

"You never come here so late unless there is something on your mind," Thomas said. "Pray, shall you disclose the matter at hand, or must we engage in a game of billiards to extract the information from you?"

Richard chuckled, shaking his head.

"It has been the most eventful day that I believe I have ever experienced," he said.

Thomas's eyebrows raised, nearly meeting his hairline.

"This sounds rather interesting," he said, pausing to sip his drink.

Richard did the same, then he began telling Thomas everything about the day. He started with Susan's surprise stop at the Huxley townhouse, and he finished by telling him about the encounter with Lady Beatrice. Thomas listened as he always did, his expression changing from shock to amusement to twitching eyebrows as Richard spoke. He looked especially interested when Richard told him of Susan's proposal. After Richard finished his tale, Thomas paused thoughtfully, sipping his drink.

The two men drank in silence for a moment before Thomas spoke again.

"I must say that your sister's idea is hardly a terrible one," he said. "That just might be the thing you need to cease your mother's endless matchmaking nonsense."

67

Richard shot his friend a sharp look, but deep down, he knew the idea wasn't entirely ludicrous to him. He had, in fact, entertained it many times that day. He supposed it made sense that Thomas might agree with Susan. He had, after all, been the one to suggest that Richard find his own bride.

"Mother would surely object," Richard said at last, shaking his head. "She is not fond of Miss Huxley at all, especially not after this morning's paper."

Thomas shrugged, looking at Richard intently.

"Should you be concerned?" he asked. "She wants you to marry. You would, by all accounts, be preparing to do just that."

Richard nodded, frowning.

"That's the other problem," he said. "Sooner or later, the courtship would have to end. What would people say about that once it did?"

Thomas shrugged again, swirling the port around in his glass.

"I say again, should you be concerned?" he repeated. "The ton members will always find something to gossip about. Besides, once the courtship ended, you might be assured that no one would ever consider marrying you, if any scandal should arise afterward."

Richard nodded, but he was still doubtful.

"But is that fair to Miss Huxley?" he asked, thinking back to his earlier concerns. "Wouldn't that jeopardise her reputation more than it would harm me?"

Thomas thought it over for a moment before nodding.

"Perhaps," he said. "But you can't know if it would be worth it to her unless you asked her if she would consider it."

Richard took another drink, thinking over what Thomas had just said. That was one thing he hadn't considered; asking Miss Huxley if she would be interested in that plan. He had been trying to think of how she would feel about it, without even thinking of bluntly taking the proposal to her. It was a long shot, and it was still a pretty wild idea. But he supposed the only way he could know her thoughts on the matter would be if he asked her outright.

"Perhaps," he murmured.

Once the men finished their drinks, Richard took his leave, making his way back home. In his chambers, as the moonlight filtered through his window, Richard thought about his duties, the freedoms he had always longed to have, and his unexpected interest in Miss Huxley. The weight of his title and the duties of which his mother kept reminding him felt as though they were suffocating him, and he couldn't believe he was even entertaining the suggestion that both Susan and Thomas seemed to think was a good one. And yet, amidst his turmoil over the dukedom duties and responsibilities, Miss Huxley kept making her way to the center of his thoughts.

With a resigned sigh, Richard summoned his valet and readied himself for bed. He was not benefiting himself by brooding over the burden and inquiries troubling his thoughts. Perhaps, if he could get a good, proper night's sleep, it would bring him the clarity about his situation that he so desperately needed.

Chapter Nine

The moment Anne's eyes opened the next morning, her heart fell into her stomach. A glance outside her window showed her another beautiful, late spring day, which was once something that always put her in good spirits. Now, however, such lovely days only taunted her with brightness and vibrancy that she could no longer access in her life. All that awaited her when she went downstairs would be a minefield of tension during the family breakfast, and constantly feeling like a pariah in her own home for the rest of the day.

Filled to the brim with dread, Anne rose and summoned Martha, idly choosing a pale-yellow dress for the day. As Martha helped her dress, she tried to convince herself that the meal wouldn't be as bad as she feared, that the anger at her from the incident at the ball two nights before would have dissipated and that, even if the conversation was somewhat stilted, it wouldn't be as unbearable as she was concerned it would be. But as she looked at herself in the mirror, she knew that wasn't true. Her parents, specifically her mother, never forgot any of her behaviors. Especially the ones that they felt made their family look bad.

As she approached the dining hall, her heart was heavy with anxiety. She put on her best pleasant smile and entered, glancing around to try to read the expressions of her family members. The scene before her was familiar, and not particularly tense. Her father sat behind his newspaper, undoubtedly browsing the business sections. Her mother held her own paper, and Anne knew without studying it that it was the scandal sheets. It was the only section of the paper she ever read, and she paid close attention lately for any news about Anne. And Charlotte sipped her coffee with a serene smile that warmed Anne's heart. As she took her seat in front of her plate full of scrambled eggs, ham and grapes, she allowed herself to think once more that meal might not be as painful as she'd feared.

But as she put the first bite of eggs to her lips, her mother firmly shoved the paper down to the level of the table, narrowing her eyes over something on the page.

"The duke of Calder was seen In Gunter's having a rendezvous with a young lady who is quite well-known within the ton for her public antics."

Anne swallowed hard, putting down the still-full fork. Even before her mother continued reading, she knew to whom the paper referred. Moreover, she knew how the gossip column had gotten their hands on such information. The women who had approached them while Susan and the Duke of Calder and she enjoyed their treats had been insulted by the way the duke brushed them off, and as revenge, they had started spreading rumors about the outing. Would that detail be in the paper, as well, placing her in the middle of another social embarrassment?

Her mother had finished reading the piece by the time Anne pulled herself from her thoughts. Both the viscount and the viscountess were looking directly at her with matching scrutinous expressions on their faces.

"Well, it appears to be a glimmer of favorable tidings," the viscount remarked at length, offering his daughter a strained smile. "It seems the duke has taken notice of you, and you haven't bungled your behaviour in his presence."

Anne blinked, confused. Was her father pleased that she had been seen with the duke?

Her mother looked her over, thinking over something very deeply.

"That seems to be a good sign," she said with a measured tone. "Truly, it sounds like something of a miracle."

Anne allowed herself to relax a little. It was backhanded praise, she knew. But it wasn't the usual shamed admonishment she typically got from her parents.

Charlotte put down her cup, her mouth hanging open.

"Sister, you didn't tell me that a duke had taken an interest in you," she said, beaming at Anne.

Anne blushed, shaking her head at her sister. She was preparing to explain that he wasn't interested in her, that their presence at Gunter's had been incidental, and all at the behest of

71

Susan. Even though it was bringing her positive attention, she didn't want anyone to get the wrong idea and get their hopes up. But before she could say a word, her father raised an eyebrow and gave her mother a look.

"A duke holds considerable influence in society," he said, sounding as guarded with his words as her mother had.

The viscountess nodded in agreement, her face suddenly solemn.

"It is quite a surprise that a duke would have an interest in spending time with our Anne," she said.

Anne looked back and forth between her parents, confused. Her mother hadn't referred to her as 'their Anne' since she was a young girl. It was a term that once brought her comfort. Now, it only filled her with uncertainty. She couldn't read their feelings about the gossip article. Usually, their displeasure was clear enough for a deaf person to hear. But right then, they were behaving as though there was something they wanted to say but weren't.

The viscount reached for the scandal sheet, which his wife dutifully handed over to him. He took a moment to read the piece for himself, and Anne dropped her eyes to her plate. Her heart was racing as she waited to see what her parents ultimately had to say. Would they, indeed, be pleased? Or would they find some embarrassing scandal in being seen in public with the Duke, even though she hadn't been alone with him?

When her father looked up at her again, his expression was a strange mix of pride and skepticism. Anne braced herself, certain she was going to be admonished.

"Well, this would appear to be a good thing for your reputation," he finally said. "And for our family, as well."

Anne wanted to be relieved by her father's words. But his tone was dubious and guarded. Anne squirmed uncomfortably in her seat. Thankfully, her sister noticed. Charlotte turned back to her, giving her a reassuring smile.

"I think it's just wonderful," she said. "Just imagine, my own elder sister a duchess someday. It's something out of a storybook."

The viscountess nodded slowly, skepticism filling her features.

"Storybook, indeed," she said. "The Duke of Calder certainly has his pick of the ton's eligible ladies. It is curious that he would consider an outing with Anne."

Anne looked at her mother in surprise. She knew she wasn't a season diamond. But she was pretty, she could hold respectable conversations with others, provided they were respectful to her, and she enjoyed playing the pianoforte and dancing. Why was it such a great surprise that any nobleman would find her interesting?

The viscount nodded, scrunching up his face as he continued surveying his middle daughter.

"Surely, he wouldn't have any interest in a lady with such a lively reputation," he said.

The blow hit Anne directly in her heart. So, that was what the truth was behind her parents' sentiments. They thought their own daughter wouldn't be good enough for a duke. Heat flushed her cheeks, and she looked away from her parents in humiliation. She was sure that only they could take something innocuous and potentially good and turn it into something to hurt or shame her.

"It does leave room to question his intentions," the viscountess said.

Tears stung Anne's eyes, but she blinked them away. She wished she would open her mouth to defend herself and point out how many people deserved shameful reputations within the ton. Her cousin, Albert, being one of them. But no defense would come. She was too wounded and stunned by the harshness of her parents' words to stand up for herself.

She glanced up at Charlotte, who was looking at her with sympathy. For her younger sister's sake, Anne forced a polite smile while pushing her eggs around her plate. She pretended to be engrossed in a meal she knew she wouldn't eat as the conversation continued around her. She wished more than anything to escape the hurtful, embarrassing scrutiny and to find solace in the quiet corners of her own thoughts. The duke had no romantic interest in her, anyway. But to hear her parents list all the reasons why he never would, made her wish the ground would remove her from the perpetual shame.

Finally, breakfast mercifully concluded. Anne quietly excused herself and then hurriedly made her escape to the drawing room. She sank into the plush armchair to the side of the large bay window, her thoughts swirling. Her face was still warm, and she knew her cheeks were bright red. How could her own family embarrass her so terribly over something that would make any other family delighted? And how could they do that right in front of her, as though she had no feelings worth considering?

She understood that things like throwing wine on someone or stomping on the toes of a man who was very fresh with her did reflect poorly on her family. But no one ever listened to her when she tried to tell someone how people disrespected her. It was as if she had to withstand any vile words or propositions directed toward her, just for the sake of propriety. And that was something she could never do.

She saw no reason why she should tolerate things that people would never tolerate from her, just because standing up for herself made her appear unladylike. And she didn't think she should be publicly shunned for accidents, like when she knocked over the champagne flutes trying to flee from Albert. And yet, that seemed to be the only things people knew about her. They were the only things anyone cared about. Was she not a human being with feelings to be considered, as well?

As she stared out the window, reliving every pointed thing her parents had said at breakfast, the butler entered the drawing room, holding a sealed note on a silver tray.

"Miss Huxley," he said, bowing and giving her a small smile. "This just arrived for you."

Anne's heart skipped a beat as she recognized Susan's handwriting. She accepted the note with a sense of anticipation, eager for a distraction from the hurt and unease her family had caused her.

"Thank you, Reeves," she said warmly.

The butler dipped his head, turning with the now empty silver tray and disappearing from the room. She tore open the letter, reading the words her friend had scrawled on the page. But as she started to read, Mischief leapt onto the nearby table, knocking over the inkwell in a comical display of his typical feline

74

chaos. Anne couldn't help but stifle a laugh as she rescued the letter from potential disaster, moving it to the side and simultaneously catching the ink well before anything more than a few droplets of ink splashed out from the top of the well.

"You silly, sweet boy," Anne said, setting the ink well out of the cat's reach and kissing him on the head. "Now, we must clean this up."

She walked over to the desk, finding an old handkerchief in the bottom drawer. She went back over to the table, wiping up the splatters of ink before they dried and stained the table. She tucked the inky cloth into the pocket of her dress, then sat back down to finish reading the letter. Mischief joined her, sitting up straight with his front paws touching daintily in front of him in his pretty boy pose, as though he was reading the letter with her.

The message was an invitation to tea from Susan. The added note that Susan's mother would be occupied with an outing with the Westbrooks filled Anne with relief. She was aware of the dowager duchess's feelings about her. They were no more flattering or kind than those of her own parents. And yet imagining the duchess's reaction to Susan's secretive correspondence brought a mischievous grin to Anne's lips. It felt much like a small victory in a world that was determined to shun and scold her at every turn.

Mischief got bored of reading the letter with his mistress, deciding instead to chase after a loose quill, and Anne's spirits lifted for the first time that day. Between her friend's invitation to tea, which would keep her away from home for a few hours, and Mischief's playful antics, Anne felt like her day might yet be salvageable. Yet in the recesses of her thoughts rose an unexpected question. Would Richard be there? The mere possibility sent her heart into a wild, erratic dance. Would he regret defending her out in public if he noticed the scandal sheets?

Chapter Ten

Richard moved silently through the long, grand halls of his family's lavish home. He knew that his mother would be busy that day with the Westbrooks, but he wanted to ensure that she was gone before showing his face anywhere on the first floor of the mansion. Not only did he not wish to have the discussion of marriage with his mother that day, but he also didn't want her to decide to drag him with her. He had no inclination to meet Lady Eleanor, just as much as he dreaded the thought of inflicting pain upon himself. So, he waited and listened for any sign that his mother was still moving about in the mansion somewhere.

As he wandered, he thought of the weight on his shoulders. It wasn't just his mother's incessant matchmaking efforts, although that preoccupied a great deal of his mind. He had tenants to oversee and collect from, he had his business ventures in his textile mill, his investments in the technology industry, and the selling of the iron that was mined by hired miners on his family's land. He also held his father's old position in the House of Lords, although he was far less engaged with parliament than many of the other dukes.

Of course, he had his steward, Davis, who helped him keep up with the affairs of the estate itself, including the mining employees and profits. And he had his employees of his other ventures who ensured that everything continued running smoothly. Still, it was overwhelming sometimes. He was aware that a duchess could take over some of the estate overseeing for him, which would alleviate his burden. But only the right duchess could do that. And women like Lady Eleanor were far from the right ones.

As he rounded a corner, he was pulled from his thoughts by the soft murmur of voices drifting gently from the second-floor drawing room. The familiar cadences of those voices instantly caught his attention, and he paused just beyond the partially open door. One of the voices was one he had known most of his life. And the other one he had heard just the day before. Susan and Miss Huxley were inside the room, speaking in hushed but urgent tones.

Richard wasn't typically one for eavesdropping, especially on the dull conversations of most ton ladies. But from the pitches of Miss Huxley's voice, it seemed the conversation was anything but boring. His curiosity was piqued, so he pressed himself against the wall, just outside the open door.

"They were just horrible," Miss Huxley was saying, emotion thick in her voice, causing it to crack. "They seemed delighted at first, when they learned that I was with your brother at Gunter's. But then, they said that a woman the likes of me could never be good enough for a duke."

There was a soft sob, which Richard knew had to have come from Miss Huxley. His heart squeezed. Why would her parents say such a thing? Other than being a little defensive and tense, she had been perfectly pleasant company. And she was hardly unattractive. Not to mention that she could carry on a substantial conversation. What would make her parents be so cruel?

"My dearest, that's nonsense," Susan said after a brief pause. "Surely, you don't believe that you're not good enough for anyone. Why, I think any man, duke or prince, would be lucky to have you."

Richard bit his lip, wondering what made him agree with his sister. Miss Huxley had been sweet and charming after she had warmed up, that was true. But he still hardly knew her. Still, he couldn't argue with Susan. And he didn't think it was right that her own family would try to tell her otherwise.

As he peeked into the room, Richard saw Susan comforting her friend, pulling her into a tender embrace. The genuine affection between the two friends tugged at Richard's heart, and he felt a surge of protectiveness and empathy for Miss Huxley, who was clearly struggling with her family's expectations. That was a plight he knew all too well. And to think of a lady as seemingly respectable and intelligent as her going through the same brought Richard an unexpected sadness.

Choosing to intervene, Richard entered the room, his unexpected presence catching both ladies off guard.

"Forgive me," he said with an apologetic smile. "I could not help overhearing what you were saying just now, Miss Huxley. In truth, I confess to standing outside the door and listening before I just barged in here. I just wanted to tell you that I understand how you must feel, what with so much unnecessary and cold pressure from your own family. I wanted to express my deepest sympathies for your predicament."

Miss Huxley's eyes widened and her face paled.

"Your Grace, forgive me," she said, wiping at her eyes with her delicate fingertips. "I never meant for you to overhear my troubles. I do apologise. Your Grace, please do not tell my parents what you heard. I'm truly sorry for having imposed upon you in this matter, however inadvertently it might have been."

Richard's heart ached as the young woman rambled with her apologies. She was clearly fearful of repercussions from her parents. As he supposed she would be, after what Susan had told him that they were trying to do to her the previous day. He pulled a handkerchief from his coat pocket, offering it to her with his warmest smile.

"You have no need to apologise," he said. "I was the one who chose to listen into your conversation uninvited. It is I who should apologise, and I do, with all my heart. I hope that you can forgive me, as I should have never done that. And fear not, I will not speak a word of what you said to anyone. Anything you say within the walls of Calder Manor is safe and will remain here with us."

Miss Huxley looked at him with wide eyes that were still tinted by fear. But as she decided she could believe what he said, relief began to take its place. She sniffled, dabbing at her eyes with the handkerchief. When she went to hand it back to him, he gently nudged her hand away.

"Keep it, please," he said. "It's the least I can do."

The emotional young woman nodded, wiping delicately at her face again. When she looked up at him, she reminded him of a wounded animal, afraid of everything and everyone, but in desperate need of care and understanding.

"Thank you, Your Grace," she said. "You are most kind. And of course, I forgive you. This is your home, after all. You've every right to hear any conversation that takes place here."

Richard nodded, impressed with Miss Huxley's demeanor. Many other ladies in the ton, Susan included, would have become infuriated with his eavesdropping and stormed off, to remain angry with him for days. But Miss Huxley was reasonable and rational, and clearly forgiving, as well. No matter what the scandal sheets, or his own mother, said about her, she carried herself with a poise and grace that most ladies in the ton lacked. At least, when she was treated with kindness, it seemed. *Exactly like that wounded animal which she appears to me,* he mused.

Susan rose then, putting her hands on her hips. Richard expected a tongue lashing from her for his eavesdropping. But what she said stunned Richard into momentary silence.

"Anne, I must tell you something," she said as though the words had just been waiting for their chance to burst from her throat. "I had an idea yesterday, and I can't wait any longer to mention it, especially after seeing you like this. I think Richard and you should have a pretend courtship."

Richard already knew of his sister's plan, of course. But the bluntness with which she had blurted it stunned him. And from the look on her friend's face, he wasn't the only one shocked at the sudden presentation.

"What?" Miss Huxley asked, her voice cracking with incredulity.

Susan turned to her friend, sitting back down, and taking her hands.

"I know it might sound crazy," she said. "But your parents are treating you horribly, and for no good reason. And they are trying to force you to marry that abysmal cousin of yours. I would prefer to be rendered sightless than to witness your nuptials with him. And Richard is facing something similar. Mother keeps trying to push that insufferable Eleanor Westbrook onto him. She would make as good a wife as I would a miner. I can't bear to see either of you suffer this way any longer."

By the time she had finished speaking, Susan's voice was also filled with raw emotion. Richard looked at his sister in surprise, but this time, it was because he hadn't known that watching his battle with their mother about marriage had affected her so badly.

Miss Huxley looked at her friend with bewilderment, clearly trying to work out what her friend was talking about.

"How would that ever work?" she asked. "A pretend courtship implies that it would have to end eventually. And I think everyone would notice when we never got married."

Susan was nodding as her friend spoke.

"They would, that is true," she said. "But by the time your courtship ended, perhaps, the two of you could have found someone you truly wish to marry. Or, at the very least, you might not be considered to be marriageable at all. Either way, you stand an excellent chance of getting out of these horrible, arranged marriages."

Richard hadn't considered the possibility of finding a woman he might be able to tolerate marrying during a pretend courtship. He still wasn't considering it then, but it was an interesting perspective. And even if he didn't, he was perfectly happy with being considered tainted or roguish after ending the fake courtship. For the first time since Susan had made her crazy proposal, Richard found himself giving it serious thought.

The silence in the room grew heavy, and Susan was looking back and forth between Miss Huxley and Richard. She bit her lip, clearly nervous and hoping they would reach the same conclusions she had about the plan. When Miss Huxley looked up at him with uncertainty and fear, Richard gave her another kind smile.

"I would like to say that I am more than happy to partake in this charade," he said. "That is, if you are, as well, Miss Huxley. I daresay that Susan has made excellent points that are difficult to dispute." He dared to give her a wink, suddenly desperate to help the wounded animal that was the lovely young woman sitting before him. "Furthermore, such a display would effectively demonstrate to your esteemed parents that you never lacked the suitable qualifications to wed a noble Duke, would it not?"

At first, Miss Huxley looked taken aback, and he feared he had taken it a step too far. But then, her eyes began searching his for sincerity. After a moment, he decided she must have believed his words genuine, for a hint of resolve washed over her face.

"It is certainly a wild plan," she said, the corners of her lips hinting at a small smile. "But I think I could participate in such a plan, as well. I will agree to this fake courtship, Your Grace."

Susan squealed, clearly teeming with excitement. She clapped her hands together, throwing her arms around her friend, who laughed at Susan's exuberance. Richard was amused as his sister's delight in their scheme, and he also wondered at himself as he found that he, too, was a little excited. Perhaps, it was the idea of finally being free from his mother's meddling. And something about Miss Huxley made him think that he would hardly have difficulty spending the time with her required to feign a courtship.

Susan released her friend, leaping up from her seat once more and rushing at Richard. He barely had enough time to lift his arms before his sister jumped into them.

"Oh, Richard, I know that neither of you will regret this," she said. "Anne is sweet, funny, and wonderful. And I know that you are compassionate, understanding, and charming. This will be a wonderful thing, I just know it. And I will help the two of you in any way I can."

Richard chuckled, returning his sister's embrace. Over her shoulder, he met Miss Huxley's eyes. They looked hopeful for the first time since he had entered the room. She blinked bashfully at him, a grateful smile spreading across her face. As he held her gaze, Richard pondered what he had just agreed to. Was it possible that he was on the path to the right decision? Or had he just made a big mistake?

Chapter Eleven

Anne sat in amazement in her friend's second-floor drawing room, the one into which they often sneaked in secret whenever the dowager duchess was at home and they didn't wish to tell her that Anne had come to visit with Susan. She hadn't had the slightest clue that her friend had been thinking of such a wild plan. She began to understand her friend's sudden arrival at her home the previous day with her brother in tow. She also understood why Susan and the duke had had such strange facial expressions when Martha and she had entered the carriage before they went to Gunter's.

But had Susan told her brother before she mentioned the plan to Anne? She studied the duke's face and decided that her friend must have at least given him a clue what she was thinking. He had hardly seemed surprised, and he had agreed rather quickly. She wasn't offended, however. It would be up to the man to make, or agree to, such an offer first, before involving a lady.

She also understood that Susan hadn't meant to leave her out or deceive her. She guessed that Susan had thought she might get her hopes up unnecessarily if she spoke to them about faking a courtship together and the duke had refused.

But he didn't refuse, she reminded herself with unexpected giddiness. She convinced herself it was due to the ambiance of the drawing room and the contagious joy of everyone else around her. But there was a small part of her that would take great satisfaction in flaunting a courtship, even a fake one, with a duke to her parents. She would love to show them that they were, in fact, wrong about her not being good enough for a duke.

And there was another small part of her that was curious to get to know the duke more. He was, indeed, very kind to even consider such a proposal, even if he would benefit from it, as well. And he had been so warm and understanding with her when he had overheard what she was saying to Susan. Perhaps, spending time with him would be more enjoyable than she had first thought when he set foot in her own drawing room the day before.

"When will our allegedly official courtship begin?" Anne found herself asking, surprised at her boldness in front of a duke. It was strange that she already felt almost as comfortable around him as she did with Susan. She told herself that it must only be because Susan was there with them. Surely, she would never be so brazen or blunt if that were not the case.

The Duke acted as though she had asked something as benign as the time or the weather. He gave her a warm, pleasant smile and shrugged.

"I believe it would be wise to delay making any formal appeals to your father or any declarations regarding our serious romantic intentions for as much time as we can," he stated. "We can arrange meetings and outings, and I can come visit you at your home, of course. But the longer we do those things, and the longer we wait to make the courtship official, the longer we can draw this out, I believe. What do you think, Miss Huxley?"

Anne nodded, unable to help smiling herself. It seemed that the duke was completely committed to ensuring that they were a believable couple. She was starting to believe that they might actually pull off their ruse. But it wasn't just that. He, as a man and a duke, had just asked for her opinion. That was unfamiliar to her, but it was certainly refreshing.

"I think that's a wonderful idea," she said.

***

The following day, Anne chose to forego breakfast with her family, pleading a megrim. She was not ill, however. She was simply consumed by her recent agreement to the staged courtship with the Duke of Calder. It felt surreal that she was going to participate in such a ruse. She had always had fanciful ideas of courtship and marriage. But the charade they were planning surpassed even those, even if it wasn't real. Her mind and heart were both reeling, and it was as overwhelming as it was empowering.

To try to settle her thoughts and emotions, she walked across her room to Mischief's basket of toys. He had been eating his breakfast, which Martha had graciously brought up for him when she brought Anne her coffee and fruit, but as soon as Anne picked up his favorite toy, an orange ribbon that had once belonged to her, he darted over to her and began batting at it before she even started letting it trail the ground.

Immediately, her pet's spirited pouncing and chasing brought her a great deal of solace. She had rescued the sweet boy from harsh weather and starvation. But it seemed he had saved her in many ways, as well. She was sure that without him, she wouldn't have been able to endure the lectures and disapproval from her parents or the gossip and cruelty of the ton. She would have wasted away into little more than a shell. But Mischief gave her purpose, and unconditional love. He was her world, and she was very thankful for him.

Eventually, however, his energy began to fade. He stopped chasing the ribbon in favor of her bringing it right to his face to bat. Then, he stretched and yawned, rubbing her legs and giving her a single meow, as if thanking her, before waddling over to his bed and curling up. As soon as she put away the ribbon, her thoughts had drifted to the Duke once again. Her stomach fluttered with both excitement and anxiety. Was she doing the right thing? Was the duke really as keen on the idea of participating in their charade as he had claimed? Or was he only doing it to appease Susan?

Later that evening, Anne, accompanied by her parents and Charlotte, left for a ball hosted by Anne's esteemed aunt Rose. As the youngest child of the previous Viscount Huxley, her grandfather, she was without a prestigious title. However, she was a notable figure within the ton, well known for her charity work, her patronage of the arts and her thriving, spectacular parties. Anne only knew her a little, but the woman had always seemed amicable enough.

Before arriving, the viscountess reached over, gripping Anne's arm tightly enough that it ached.

"I hope I needn't remind you that you are to be on your best behaviour tonight," she said. "Only impeccable behaviour is acceptable from you this evening."

Anne blushed, as much from frustration as from embarrassment.

"Yes, Mother," she said. Ordinarily, she would have stewed over such a remark all evening. But she reminded herself of her ruse with the duke, and that settled her down quickly. Her sister reached out and took her hand, giving her a sad, sympathetic look. Anne shook her head, smiling warmly back at her sister.

"It's all right," she mouthed to her younger sister. And she truly believed that it was.

However, as her family and she stepped into the lavishly decorated ballroom, many of the guests turned to watch them. To watch her, to be more specific. It didn't take long for the murmurs about her newfound association with the Duke of Calder to begin, and her previous confidence began to wane. It wasn't the worst way she had started a social event. But the disapproving and disdainful looks she kept getting told her that she was the only one who thought so. Clearly, other people in the ton were of the same opinion as her parents; that she didn't belong with a duke. She supposed they were right. She wasn't with him, and she never would be, not truly. But if they believed she was, even for a little while, she could take joy in their confusion and disbelief.

She glanced around, hoping to spot the duke somewhere in the crowd. She didn't know what he would expect of her as far as her part in their ruse when they were in public. But she thought if she could make her presence visible to him, he would take the lead so that she could play along. What she found, however, was the gaze of Lord Gray from across the room. His scowl told her that he hadn't forgotten their last encounter. That was fine by her, especially since the ton now thought she was becoming involved with the Duke. But would he try to make more trouble for her that evening? Everything was so uncertain, and Anne wished she could just run and hide.

The evening began with the first dance. Anne was thrilled when Charlotte was whisked to the dance floor right away, silently celebrating her sister. Anne noticed that her parents exchanged approving, relieved looks, and she guessed they were thinking that Charlotte might still have a chance yet at a good marriage, even despite Anne's reputation. She realized that was another bonus to her pretending to court the duke; that other men of higher, more prestigious titles and stations would take notice of Charlotte and hopefully, take an interest in her. Anne waited patiently, thinking that at any moment, the Duke would ask her to dance and begin the first big play in the game they were presenting to all of London.

As the night unfolded, however, dance after dance transpired without an invitation from the duke. She had spotted him out on the dance floor a few times, never dancing with the same woman twice. She began to second guess her decision to take part in the scheme. It seemed he wasn't interested in helping the ton believe they were interested in each other. And the relentless gossip of the people around her who had also taken note of his many dance partners and his apparent dismissal of her only fueled that doubt. Was he changing his mind about the arrangement, after all?

Just as Anne was beginning to plan a secret escape out into her aunt's gardens, Susan rushed up to her, kissing her cheek.

"Shall we go to the refreshment tables?" she asked, pointedly looking at Anne's parents, who she was well aware hadn't left her side.

Anne was confused and frustrated as to why the Duke hadn't asked her to dance yet, and with her friend for making the silly suggestion to pretend to court in the first place. But when the viscountess opened her mouth to object, Anne turned to her friend with fire in her eyes and honey in her voice.

"I'd love to," she said.

She allowed Susan to drag her to the refreshment tables all the way across the long, broad ballroom. When they reached the table, Anne turned to Susan, resisting the urge to put her hands on her hips.

"What is happening?" she hissed, trying to ignore the new stares and refreshed gossip about her continued abandonment by the duke who was supposedly smitten with her. "Why hasn't your brother danced with me yet? People are gossiping, but about the wrong thing."

Susan gave her a smug smile.

"Anne, please, trust me," she said. "All will be well. You just need to be patient for a little while longer."

Anne was fuming. She had been patient long enough, and all she had managed to do was look a fool to everyone present, despite having done nothing to embarrass herself or her family that evening. But precisely when she was poised to deliver a stern reprimand to Susan and commence indulging in immoderate libations, a spectral presence materialized behind her. Simultaneously, the first strands of a romantic waltz began as the musicians prepared to play the song.

"Miss Huxley, would you do me the tremendous honour of sharing this waltz with me?" The Duke asked, his voice dripping with charm and honey that made her knees weak, despite her previous anger.

She turned to see that his hand was already extended. She looked into his eyes, from which he was giving her a clear, pointed look that seemed to suggest that he had a plan. Relieved to be away from her parents and glad that it didn't seem as though he had reneged on their arrangement, after all, she gave him a smile.

"You have finally decided to share a dance with me?" she asked. "I think the entire ballroom had decided you weren't going to do any such thing."

The duke gave her an impish grin and a wink that melted her.

"I imagine that us dancing this waltz will give them plenty to chatter about," he said.

Suddenly, she thought she understood. He had intentionally danced with other women to keep the ton guessing. They weren't officially courting, and thus, he was enjoying himself. But for their one dance to be as passionate as the waltz would show everyone what his intentions were for Anne. She could imagine the expressions on her parents', the dowager duchess's and Lady Eleanor's faces as they spun around the dance floor doing the waltz. The image tickled her, and she began to laugh for the first time in what felt like ages. It was a genuine, true laugh, coming from a place within her that was suddenly filled with unrestrained joy. It seemed that the duke had a little lively spirit in him, too. And she found it positively delightful.

"I apologise for ever doubting you, Your Grace," she said.

Chapter Twelve

Richard felt an acute jolt of awareness shoot through him as Miss Huxley placed her hand in his. He gave her a charming smile, even though everything inside him was reeling in chaos. He had found himself strangely captivated by her when they were at Gunter's after listening to the way she spoke and seeing her smile. But as their hands held one another as he led her onto the dance floor, he felt as though he was truly seeing her for the first time.

Their first steps onto the dance floor were marked by the soft rustle of her rich pink gown. The rest of the world seemed to blur around them, and for that moment, they were the only two people in existence. As the first strains of the waltz began to play, Miss Huxley looked up at Richard, her cheeks turning the same shade as her dress. Richard gave her a small wink, leading her in getting into position. And when she smiled softly at him again, his heart skipped a beat. She was beautiful. And he felt honored to share a dance with her. Especially a waltz.

The world around them slowly came back into focus for Richard. He was acutely aware of all the judgmental eyes of the members of the ton in attendance that night focused directly on Miss Huxley and him. And he could see in Miss Huxley's eyes that she was, as well. He wanted to look up at the clusters of dancers closest to them and glower at them until they directed their eyes back to their own partners. But he was sure that would only draw more attention to them than they were already receiving.

As the dance continued, a memory resurfaced. The sound of the genuine joy in Miss Huxley's laughter earlier in the evening resonated in the back of his mind, even as the music threatened to drown it out. He had noticed the musical quality of her laughter the previous day. But when she'd laughed as they started their dance, he realized that it wasn't just musical and delicate. There was a rawness and realness to her laugh that was rare to Richard. In fact, he couldn't recall ever hearing a more sincere laugh with any of the other young women he'd ever encountered within the ton. All the others only giggled and laughed when they were trying to seduce a man to marry. But Miss Huxley clearly had joy in her soul, even with the way the ton gossiped about her. He realized that he wanted to hear her laugh more frequently.

As they waltzed past a group of women who were staring at the two of them with sour expressions on their faces at the very edge of the dance floor, Richard gave her an impish grin. He gave a little swish of his coat tail so that it flew out and gently bumped one of the women. She gasped, causing Richard's smile to widen. And when Miss Huxley realized what had happened, she laughed again.

"They'll be talking about that, for sure," she said, her jade green eyes dancing with merriment.

Richard shrugged. He entertained doubts that they would retain such a trivial offence, particularly considering the high probability that the lady had encountered the bristle rather than experiencing its physical impact. But he didn't care. It had been a very subtle gesture to shun the disapproving looks the women had been giving Miss Huxley. And it had made her laugh again. To him, it was all well worth it.

"Talking about what?" he asked, putting on a grand show of feigning innocence.

The young woman in his arms laughed again, and a shiver ran up his spine. It was as if divine wine ran through his blood with her every giggle, and he felt dizzy with intoxication. He knew he would do anything he could, for as long as he could, to hear her laugh every chance he got.

The waltz came to an end all too soon, and Richard couldn't hide his disappointment. But he gave her another broad smile as he offered his arm to escort her off the dance floor.

"You dance very gracefully, Miss Huxley," he said.

Her cheeks flushed and she gave him a shy smile.

"Thank you, Your Grace," she said. "You are a wonderful dancer, as well."

Richard smiled at her, dipping his head slightly.

"Thank you, Miss Huxley," he said, captivated by how much lovelier she was when her cheeks turned pink. "But only if I have a good dancing partner. Which you most certainly were."

She blushed again, but her smile widened.

"I've never danced the waltz before," she said. "Not outside my dancing lessons when I was a girl."

Richard gave her a look of sincere approval.

"Well, then you deserve still more praise," he said. "You danced it like natural tonight."

She grinned at him, and he masked the emptiness he felt at having to leave her company by keeping his own smile. He bowed to her once they reached the other side of the ballroom, and she curtseyed in return.

"I hope to see you again this evening," he said truthfully.

Miss Huxley looked surprised, but she nodded with another small smile.

"That would be lovely, Your Grace," she said.

As they parted ways, the hushed murmurs of gossip concerning their dance became audible. The ever-judgmental ton had made them the evening's focal point, and without her smile and laugh to distract him from the weight of so much attention fixed firmly on him, he suddenly wanted to flee the ballroom. He realized, as he had with his sudden infatuation with her laugh, that he admired Miss Huxley right then. She, too, had been aware of all the eyes on them. And yet, she had carried herself with all the poise and grace of a noblewoman of a much higher status.

As he reflected on the evening and the woman he was soon to pretend to court, his thoughts were abruptly interrupted by a voice that caused him to shudder.

"Miss Huxley?" Sebastian Gray said with a chortle. "Surely you merely took pity on her. After all, she did receive quite an unflattering piece in the scandal sheets." The man snorted. "Again."

Richard took a long, slow breath. He had expected for people to whisper about the two of them. What he hadn't expected was for someone to approach him and try to cause trouble with a duke at a ball. He turned slowly to face Lord Gray, giving him a playful smirk.

"Are you jealous that I earned her attention?" he quipped.

Lord Gray's expression dropped as he studied Richard's face for a hint of seriousness. Then, he snickered once more.

"Hardly," he said, examining his perfectly groomed fingernails as though bored. "I would never get myself involved with a woman who was so well-known for her past... antics."

Richard bristled. He had found Miss Huxley perfectly delightful, as well as kind and witty. And even though he didn't have a real interest in her love, he didn't feel that he should let someone get away with saying such things about her.

"It's interesting how everyone enjoys the scandal sheets, until they find themselves being discussed there," he said with an overly sweet smile. "It would be a shame to be the next one to find your name there for stirring up your own 'antics,' wouldn't it?"

At that, Lord Gray's face fell completely, anger flashing in his eyes. The tension between the men was palpable, but Richard wouldn't allow slander to mar Miss Huxley's name any more than it already had. He stood firm, ready to protect her honor at any cost.

After a long moment of attempting to intimidate Richard with a glaring contest, Sebastian Gray turned on his heel, giving Richard the satisfaction of watching him storm off in a huff. With a sigh of relief, he made his way to the side of the ballroom, where the door to the terrace was open. When he stepped outside, he heard another familiar voice; this one far more welcomed and appreciated.

"Excellent timing, Richard," Thomas said, holding up a cigar and grinning. "I was just thinking about how lonesome it would be to stand out here and smoke alone."

Grateful for the reprieve, Richard grinned, pulling a cigar from his own pocket. The men lit their cigars and Richard took a long, satisfying pull from his. As his nerves began to settle, he looked at Thomas and shook his head.

"This is just what I needed, I believe," he said. "These people with their incessant gossip will be the death of me."

Thomas laughed again and looked over Richard's shoulder at what he knew had to be a ballroom full of people looking in his direction.

"Yes," he said. "It seems that your dance with Miss Huxley has caused quite a buzz."

Richard grinned, lifting his cigar.

"Good," he said in the hopes that one of the nosy gossips might overhear. "And they'll see plenty more of it in the coming weeks."

The men shared a laugh, and Richard finally felt the tension from the evening melting away. And as Thomas and he smoked their cigars and made their own little snide remarks about the gossips of London, he found himself having a pleasant time.

However, he knew there would be a problem the second he helped his mother and sister into the carriage that evening when they were headed home. The dowager duchess's eyes were ablaze and locked firmly onto his face.

"I suppose you know what the scandal sheets will say tomorrow," she said, her voice clipped and dripping with disapproval. "You didn't even dance with Eleanor."

Richard shrugged, a pounding beginning at his temples.

"I didn't see her," he lied, holding his mother's gaze. "And what will the scandal sheets say, Mother? That I had a lovely dance with a lovely woman?""

His mother scoffed, shaking her head in complete disbelief.

"Lovely?" she asked. "That woman could ruin your reputation. Has your judgment truly become so impaired that you can't see that? Why would you dance with her, knowing that everyone would see?"

The atmosphere in the carriage was becoming increasingly oppressive. Even though it was a pleasantly cool night, it felt as though it was becoming hard to breathe. He had known that his mother wouldn't be thrilled with him dancing with Miss Huxley. But he would have expected her to have less to say about it, at least since there was no scene made.

"Mother, the ton is always gossiping about something," he said, feeling frustrated all over again. "Whether one gives them a reason or not, they find reasons."

His mother looked at him as though he had just suggested right then that he marry Miss Huxley.

"That doesn't mean you should stoke the flames of gossip, Richard," she snapped. "Truly, I don't believe your judgment could be any worse these days."

93

Richard scoffed, but he said nothing else. He glanced at his sister, thinking that she might come to his defense. But she stared silently out the window, saying nothing. Richard couldn't blame her. Their mother was just as hard on Susan about her time spent with Miss Huxley. But hadn't it been all her idea for them to enter into a pretend courtship? If Susan wasn't going to help him when their mother became difficult when the subject at hand was Miss Huxley, how could he ever convince his mother that he intended to marry her, gossip and the opinions of others aside?

Chapter Thirteen

The moment Anne's eyes were open the next morning, her thoughts went straight to the evening before. Specifically, the waltz she had shared with the Duke. Her parents had said nothing to her about it the previous evening. She wondered if they would be as unhappy about it as they would be over any other alleged spectacle she could have caused. She supposed that would all depend on what the scandal sheets said. But surely, no one could take away something bad from a dance that had gone very well and that they had both seemed to enjoy, right?

She smiled as she thought about how he brushed his coat tail against the group of women close to the dance floor. His blue eyes had sparkled brilliantly with mischief that was as genuine as it was harmless. If she hadn't known better, she would have thought he enjoyed being a little impish. He was certainly handsome, that much she couldn't deny. And the more time she spent with him, the more she saw kindness and charm in him, as well.

However, her inner voice reminded her that her relationship with the duke was nothing more than a ruse. However sweet, charming and mischievous he might be, he was only in her life to prevent the two of them from ending up married to people they couldn't stand. There was the potential for friendship, she was sure. In some ways, the duke was a bit like his sister. But that was all they would ever be. She supposed she could do worse than to have such a man as her friend. But she couldn't let herself get swept away in the fantasy of a shared life with him when no such thing could ever come to pass.

"Miss Huxley?" Martha asked from the doorway, startling her. "Are you ready to dress for breakfast now?"

Anne looked at her lady's maid, blushing. She hadn't heard the maid come in, and she laughed nervously.

"Yes, I suppose I am," she said, motioning the maid to come inside as she swung her legs over the side of the bed. As far as she knew, she had no plans for that day. She decided that she would wear a simple orange day dress and have Martha style her hair in a simpler bun that was held in place by rhinestone studded hair pins. She hardly felt the need to dress spectacularly when she didn't expect any company or intend to leave her home that day.

As her maid helped her dress, she noticed that Martha kept stealing glances at her. She was sure she could guess why. But she went ahead and asked the maid, anyway.

"What's wrong?" she asked.

Martha glanced at the door, which was firmly shut.

"It's the scandal sheets," she whispered. "Seems you're in them yet again."

Anne took a deep breath. She had been expecting it. But if Martha was acting sneaky, that couldn't mean anything good where her parents were concerned.

"What have Mother and Father said?" she asked reluctantly.

Martha shrugged.

"I've not heard a word from them," she said. "I only heard Miss Charlotte mention something about you dancing with a dashing duke."

Anne smiled again at the thought of Richard.

"I certainly did," she said. "But we are only friends who plan to help one another escape horrible marriages with worse people."

Martha's eyes widened as Anne explained their ruse quickly and quietly. Her lady's maid was grinning by the time she was dressed and ready for breakfast, putting an arm around her shoulders.

"That's lovely to hear," she said. "Now, you needn't worry yourself with that awful cousin of yours."

Anne nodded, but there was a shred of disappointment. She knew she could never consider the duke a true option for marriage for her. But did it hurt to entertain the thought sometimes, if only silently to herself?

She went downstairs, sensing the anticipation in the air before she reached the open door to the breakfast room. The paper lay on the table, but three pairs of eyes were focused squarely on her. She swallowed, entering the room timidly and taking her seat. Was the scandal sheet truly that bad this time?

Her mother studied her, her eyes filled with questions and her mouth not forming a single one. And her father kept glancing

96

from the paper back to her, making her squirm. *I think I should like another lecture instead of this,* she thought as her cheeks grew hot. What could the paper say that would make her family so quiet?

Charlotte was the one who finally broke the silence. Her expression, unlike those of their parents, was clearly excited. She reached out and pulled the paper to her, only to press it into Anne's hands immediately after.

"Sister, look," she gushed, her eyes sparkling with mischief, much like the Duke's had the night before. "Everyone is dying to know more about your dance with the Duke last night."

Anne skimmed the scandal sheet piece, her heart racing as she looked for anything she had done that was unflattering or for which her parents might be upset. But each word in the piece was as kind as the scandal sheets ever were to any noble man or woman, and indeed, only centered around the dance and the pair's recent interactions. Anne wanted to breathe a sigh of relief. But her parents were still watching her with a guarded wariness that Anne couldn't understand. Why would they not at least say something to her about the night before? Even if they were furious?

"I see," Anne said, testing her voice to see if it worked.

"Well, aren't you going to tell me all about it?" Charlotte asked, bouncing in her seat. "It was all anyone could talk about last night."

Anne shrugged. She knew she had to answer carefully until she could explain to Charlotte what was truly happening. She couldn't mention anything about marriage when they hadn't even officially begun their fake courtship. But nor could she be too casual about the dance. She wondered if there was a right answer, with as strangely as her parents were behaving.

"It was a very lovely dance," she said, trying to sound light and carefree, but not telling. "He is very charming and witty, and he said I was a very graceful dancer."

Her parents looked from her back to one another, and Anne feared she would go mad. After a long, silent exchanged look between the viscount and the viscountess, the silence was finally broken once more.

"Well, in light of these circumstances, perhaps, we can halt the plans for your union to Albert," her father said.

Anne was grateful to have not touched any food as she knew she would have choked. She knew that was the whole point of her plan with Richard. She just hadn't expected it to work so quickly.

Knowing that her father would be expecting a reaction and a response, she looked up at him, hoping she didn't look as terrified as she felt.

"Thank you, Father," she said.

The viscountess looked at Anne again, and this time Anne understood what she saw in her mother's eyes. There was a mix of hope and anxiety there, and she even offered Anne the first smile she had seen on her mother's face since she was a child, albeit a very small one.

"This is a very interesting turn of events," she said, glancing from the scandal sheets and then back to Anne. "And I agree with your father. Should things continue between the Duke of Calder and you, he would make a far better husband for you than your cousin. You just must ensure that you do not squander this unforeseen miracle."

Anne's mind was in a whirl. She had been fearful of invoking her parents' wrath. However, instead they were quite taken with the notion that the Duke of Calder might genuinely find her captivating after merely one dance in their company. She thought back to the things they'd said about how a man of his prestige would surely never take an interest in her. Her emotions were a flurried mess, and she thought she might swoon.

When Charlotte began chattering away happily at the thought of having a duchess for a sister, Anne was more than glad to let her. It was a strange sight, to see her parents not looking at her with nothing but disappointment and disapproval. Even her father offered her a smile of his own, although he didn't say anything else to her. She wondered if he felt ashamed of the mean things he had said the day before. But deep down, she doubted it.

After breakfast, Anne excused herself as quickly as she reasonably could, anxious to get away from her parents and be alone with her thoughts. She found herself in the drawing room, the glossy keys of the pianoforte inviting her to find peace and comfort there from the morning's overwhelming revelations.

She sat on the freshly polished bench, caressing the keys with reverence. It had been ages since she played, and right then she thought that would be just the thing to quiet her wild thoughts and soothe her rattled nerves. She closed her eyes, pressing the first few notes from the waltz from the night before. She smiled, letting her hands find the chords as she began to play.

Her fingers moved gracefully across the keys, creating a lively tune that filled the room. And as the music flowed, the renewed memory of the waltz with Richard roamed free in her mind. She distinctly remembered the feel of his firm, gloved grip, their synchronized movements, and the undeniable connection that had briefly isolated them from the rest of the ton. And the way he had smiled at her when she laughed could have made anyone think that they had a genuine interest in one another.

Beneath the grand instrument where she sat, she could feel Mischief begin to play around her feet. He pounced at unseen shadows and swatted at the hem of her dress which ruffled and rustled with each tap of her foot on the pianoforte peddles. Anne laughed, shaking her head as she kept playing. She pictured Mischief dancing along to the waltz in a little suit of his own, and soon she was having to force herself to concentrate on the music as she played.

She was vaguely aware of a presence behind her as Mischief untangled himself from the hem and skirt of her dress and meandered out from beneath the bench of the pianoforte. From the smell of the perfume, Anne guessed it was her mother, so she simply kept playing while watching what Mischief was going to do. He had jumped up onto the back of the pianoforte and become very interested in his tail.

She saw what was going to happen too late to stop it. Mischief's tail flicked, drawing his eyes to it as he balanced precariously beside one of her mother's prized, unique flower vases that was full of fresh gardenias. He dove for his tail which had ended up curled around the base of the vase. It teetered for a single second before it fell, crashing to the floor with a hollow thud. Anne was relieved that it hadn't broken, but the flowers and water spilled, narrowly missing the back of the pianoforte. She grabbed the cat with amazing nimbleness, preparing to chastise him in her typical gentle fashion.

"Anne, that cat of yours nearly ruined yet another priceless item," her mother bellowed.

Anne and Mischief both winced, and Anne held him tightly to her so that he wouldn't escape and make matters worse. But before either of them could say anything further, the butler rushed into the room.

"The Duke of Calder has arrived to call on Miss Anne," he said, his voice almost too calm in the echo of her mother's reprimand.

Every nerve in Anne's body felt electrified. She pushed her disheveled hair back and straightened her dress, attempting to gather her composure. And then, Richard stepped into the room, carrying a bouquet of pink roses. Her favorite flowers.

"Good morning, Lady Huxley and Miss Huxley," he said with a charming smile that sent a rush of warmth through her veins. "I do hope I'm not intruding."

Anne stood feeling as dumbfounded as her mother looked. What was he doing there? And how had he guessed pink roses, of all flowers, to bring to her?

Chapter Fourteen

It was clear to Richard that he had, indeed, interrupted something between Miss Huxley and her mother. Miss Huxley looked like a frightened doe and the viscountess looked angry, bewildered and baffled. And at the center of it all was a ball of orange fur, almost the same color as Miss Huxley's dress. It was squirming in her grasp, and she looked both worried and helpless to keep the animal still. Richard looked down at the ground, where a maid was now dabbing and picking up some damp flowers and he understood what must have happened. The cat appeared to have knocked over a vase full of flowers. And by the look on the viscountess's face, she was far from impressed.

The younger Huxley daughter entered the room just then, her lips parted as if to say something. But the second her eyes landed on Richard, she curtseyed. The gesture brought the viscountess back to her senses, and she copied her younger daughter in a perfect curtsey.

"Good morning, Your Grace," Miss Charlotte said. With a glance at her sister, who was notably more disheveled looking than she herself and their mother did, she continued. "Shall Mother and I have tea summoned for you?"

Upon hearing her youngest daughter speak, the viscountess put on a wide smile.

"Yes, let us do that, darling," she said, her voice clearly strained as she gave Miss Anne a sour look. "We'll see to tea right now, Your Grace." Miss Charlotte and she signaled for tea, which Richard acknowledged rather quickly.

"Yes, thank you," he murmured. He raised his eyebrow, trying not to laugh at the cat, which was still wriggling in his mistress's arms. He held out the flowers to Miss Anne, giving her a bemused smile.

"If this is a bad time, I could come back another day," he said.

Miss Anne glanced up at where her mother and sister were speaking with another maid, shaking her head firmly.

"That's quite all right," she said nervously. "This is a nice, pleasant surprise, Your Grace."

Richard bit his tongue to keep from pointing out that it looked to be the worst surprise in that moment. The two of them stood in awkward silence for a long moment, and Richard tried to think of something to say to lighten up the mood a little.

"Would you like for me to put these in a vase for you?" he asked.

Miss Anne blushed furiously, shaking her head and freeing one of her hands from the squirming cat.

"Oh, forgive me," she said, holding out her hand to meet his. "No, it is quite alright. I shall request one of the servants to attend to it."

Richard nodded, surprised at how endearing she looked to him with her flushed cheeks and flustered appearance. She took the flowers, but not before their hands brushed against each other. A sudden surge of electric sensation coursed through his limb, and settled in his heart and stomach, lingering even after he had pulled his hand away from hers. The quiet tension increased as they stood there staring at each other. Richard had never tried courting any of the ton ladies before, but he was sure that none of them had ever even won a true, genuine smile from him. So, how was it that Miss Anne was having such a strange effect on him?

"How did you know that I like pink roses?" she finally asked, breaking the silence.

From the doorway where they both still stood, Richard noticed that Miss Charlotte and Lady Huxley both looked at Anne when she spoke. Her sister looked as amused as he felt, but their mother looked like she was minutes away from a lecture. Miss Anne blushed again, biting her lip before speaking again. "I mean, they are lovely. They're my favourite, in fact. I was just curious as to what made you choose those."

Richard gave her a reassuring smile, pointedly ignoring her mother as he spoke to her.

"Susan told me," he said. "I thought that since the two of you have been friends for so long, she might be able to help me with flowers for you. I'm glad you like them."

102

Miss Anne returned his smile with a small, grateful one of her own as she nodded.

"I love them," she said, her voice soft and delicate, not at all as confident and strong as it had been at Gunter's or at the ball the night before. "Thank you, Your Grace."

Richard bowed, still remembering the lightning sensation when their hands had touched.

"It's my pleasure, truly," he said.

Mischief, sensing that his mistress was distracted right then and choosing to live up to his name, wriggled free from Miss Anne's embrace at last. He landed deftly on the floor with all four feet and curiously approached Richard. The cat, with his sleek orange fur, inspected his polished shoes before affectionately rubbing against his trousers, leaving a trail of fur in his wake. Richard couldn't help but smile, feeling an unexpected fondness for the playful feline.

"Anne, my dear," the viscountess said. Her tone had softened, but one look at her eyes showed Richard the disapproving glare she was giving her middle daughter and the feline. "Won't you have Mischief taken to your chambers and kept there before he can make any more trouble?"

Miss Anne flushed again, and she reached down to grab the cat. But Richard picked him up first, holding him to his chest and earning himself a few more strands of orange fur on his jacket to match his pants.

"That's perfectly all right, my lady," Richard said, again not looking at the viscountess as he addressed her. "I like animals. And he's done nothing to offend me since I arrived." *Indeed, I reckon he is endeared to me, as time passes,* he added silently, marveling at the fast connection not only with Miss Anne, but her rambunctious feline companion, as well.

The viscountess looked as though she hadn't expected such understanding from him. But she plastered on a big smile and led the maids, who had returned with trays of tea and cakes, over to where Richard and Miss Anne still stood. Miss Anne gave him another sweet smile of gratitude, wincing apologetically toward her cat.

"I'm sorry," she mouthed.

103

Richard shook his head, scratching the cat behind the ears and earning him a brief moment of purring.

"No harm done," he mouthed back.

He gently put the cat, who raced to join his mistress while he continued to survey Richard closely, back down on the ground. Then, he took a seat on a two-seating bench, across from Miss Anne's mother and sister. Miss Anne sat down beside him, idly scratching her pet, and Richard was glad to see that she was beginning to relax a little.

"Well, it certainly seems like our little Mischief likes you," Miss Charlotte said with a giggle. "Do you have any pets?"

The viscountess's expression soured again, but she didn't say anything, opting instead to sip her tea. Richard shook his head, glancing down at Mischief, who had temporarily become distracted by a loose ribbon on Miss Anne's dress.

"I have no cats or dogs," he said. "Although, I do have horses, and I love them. I like animals, though. They keep things interesting. To be sure."

Miss Charlotte giggled, gazing at the cat fondly.

"That's one way of looking at it," she said.

Miss Anne gave her sister a playful glare.

"He's a good cat," she said. "He's just still young and playful."

The viscountess gave Miss Anne another of her warning looks. But she simply looked at Richard and smiled.

"Did you come calling on Anne to invite her somewhere today?" she asked.

Richard shook his head, beginning to feel irate with how cold and harsh the viscountess sounded when speaking to and about her own daughter.

"Not today, my lady," he said. "I have an important business meeting this evening." He paused, turning to Anne. "I did want to know if you would do me the honour of accompanying me to the promenade tomorrow, though."

Miss Anne looked genuinely surprised, as though she hadn't been expecting such an invitation. She appeared to be thinking it over, and Richard was happy to let her take whatever time she needed to answer him. Before she could, however, the viscountess interjected with a too-wide smile that reminded Richard a great deal of his own mother when she was calculating and plotting.

"The honour would be hers, Your Grace," she said, seemingly cornering Miss Anne into compliance. The air grew heavier with unspoken words as Miss Anne stared at her mother with reddened cheeks. Richard could see that there was something she desperately wanted to say, but she was biting her tongue. He could also see precisely what Susan had meant about how pushy and controlling the viscount and viscountess were. At least, when it came to Miss Anne. Miss Charlotte, it seemed, got far less of their parents' criticism. Richard didn't want Miss Anne to think that he pitied her. But part of him did, because he understood how that felt.

"Yes," Miss Anne said at last, giving him a weak smile. "I would be delighted."

Richard grinned, hoping to show that it was her word he was waiting for and not her mother's before responding.

"Wonderful," he said. "I shall be looking forward to it.

With tea nearly finished and Miss Anne clearly mortified at the way her mother was behaving, Richard considered leaving. But it was as though the viscountess could see or sense his readiness to leave, as she quickly rose and clasped her hands together in front of her.

"Your Grace, I was just thinking that you might like to hear a little pianoforte music," she said, her voice suddenly dripping with all the honey in London. "Our Anne is a wonder with music, and I'm sure she would be thrilled to entertain you."

Richard started to shake his head, knowing very well why her mother would want to force her to perform for him. But at this suggestion, Miss Anne looked relieved. She rose from her seat, giving him another apologetic look as she hurried past him and to the pianoforte bench, sitting down and carefully looking at the sheet music on the stand. Richard said nothing to protest her playing for him. But he held his breath, certain that she would be about as much of a 'wonder' with the pianoforte as Mischief would be.

He was once more surprised by Miss Anne, however. It seemed as though she hardly had to touch the keys to make the instrument play the sweetest notes Richard had ever heard. And the serenity on her face belied all the anxiety and tension that had been weighing her down just a short time before. Clearly, she enjoyed playing. And Richard enjoyed hearing her play.

As Anne's delicate fingers danced across the keys, the room filled with the sweet melodies of a Beethoven composition. Mischief, seemingly sensing the tranquility in the room, clambered onto Richard's lap. Caught off-guard, chuckled softly, patting the animal's head. He allowed the cat to settle in, his contented purring adding to the room's newfound tranquility. Even the viscountess didn't look reproachfully at the feline. Although Richard suspected that was because she was more interested in how impressed he was with her middle daughter.

Richard's eyes remained fixed on Anne as she played, her passion evident in every note. He was, in fact, rather impressed by Miss Anne Huxley. He found himself increasingly captivated by her, as her beauty and grace were undeniable. Her soul shone through in the way she clearly loved her pet, as well. Yet, an inner reminder nagged at him. He wasn't there to truly try courting Miss Anne. Their seemingly budding romance was nothing more than a charade. And he knew he would do well to remember that.

Chapter Fifteen

For a moment, Anne was swept in the way of the magic of playing the pianoforte. The tension in her family's home, Mischief's close call with her mother's vase, and even the duke didn't exist. It was just her and the music, and she was happy to get swept up in the joy and passion of it all. It felt like the music was caressing all her raw nerves and soothing the parts of her mind that remained constantly anxious since her parents had started to try to pressure her to marry her cousin. Mischief was healing to her soul, and music settled her most troublesome thoughts.

She was only brought back to reality when her Beethoven piece concluded, and the drawing room fell into complete silence as the final notes lingered around her. She glanced around to see that her sister's mouth had fallen open and her mother's gaze was fixed firmly onto the duke, who was staring intently at Anne. She held her breath, knowing that whatever he said would determine her own mother's words and mood.

"I am in awe, Miss Anne," the Duke finally said, his words and eyes full of genuine admiration. "Your musical skills rival those of professional musicians. I have never heard such talent apart from on a stage."

Anne's cheeks flushed hot, but for the first time in as long as she could remember, it wasn't because she felt ashamed or embarrassed. The duke was giving her sincere praise, and it both humbled and elated her. Even her mother seemed pleased, giving her a small smile. Perhaps, the rest of the day wouldn't be filled with the weight of her parents' silent admonishment, as was so often the case.

"Would you consider staying for lunch?" the viscountess asked, once more directing her attention to the duke.

The delight Anne had taken in the praise from the duke dissolved instantly in the face of the desperation in her mother's voice. She glanced over at the Duke, who was giving an indulgent smile to the viscountess as he rose, shaking his head.

"I regret being forced to say no," he said. "But I do have that meeting." He paused, turning back to Anne, his expression warming as soon as their eyes met, and he gave her a wink. "However, I shall be looking forward to promenade hour tomorrow."

Anne nodded, giving the duke what she was sure must have been her hundred thousandth grateful look. As he bowed, his cheeks turned pink, and only then did she realize that he had repeated himself when talking about taking her to the park during promenade hour. She bit her lip, hiding an amused smile. He seemed as awkward with their interactions as she was sometimes. And there was something endearing to her about that.

"As will I, Your Grace," she said shyly, with a great deal more sincerity than she'd felt after her mother had accepted the outing before she could reject it. She reminded herself that he was good company. And he seemed to feel the same way about her. She knew they needed to make their charade believable. But Anne was sure that he wouldn't be so genuine and kind to her if there wasn't some sincere interest in sharing his time with her. And if that were the case, at least she could be comfortable and have fun with him.

The viscountess and Charlotte rose to curtsey, and Anne automatically followed suit as the butler arrived to escort the duke to the door. As he exited the room, he gave her another playful smile, making her blush again. Anne remained standing even once he was gone. She wanted a moment to herself to process everything from that morning. She had been seeking that after breakfast. But now, she had even more to consider.

She was so overwhelmed with the day so far that she jumped when her mother rushed over and embraced her.

"Anne, did you see how taken he was by your performance?" she asked. "Why, anyone could see how smitten he is becoming with you. This is a promising development, darling. I am very proud of you, Anne. But being asked to promenade hour with a duke is a very big event. We must ensure you are dressed impeccably."

Anne's heart sank, diluting the marginal excitement she was beginning to feel at the idea of spending time with Richard the following day. The last thing she wanted was to feel like she was being showcased for the world to see. It was the pressure and expectations of the ton that made her uncomfortable at social events. Now, she was being put on display, exactly as she hated.

Yet, she held back her reservations, knowing how important this event was for her family's standing in society. Especially hers. It was hurtful and irritating that her mother was only proud of her now that a duke seemed to be showing interest in her. But she was grateful for the reprieve from the worry of walking into a room where her mother sat and getting more lectures or disapproving looks. If the cost for such peace was a few more social events, she supposed she could manage that.

"Oh, heavens, we will need Elizabeth's help," the viscountess said, her eyes widening. "The two of you are precisely the same measurements. And I know that your current wardrobe doesn't have the perfect gown for tomorrow. But I am certain that Elizabeth will."

Anne sighed. She felt sure it would have been enough for her to find something in her own dresser. She knew she had some new dresses she hadn't yet had any cause to wear. But she also knew that her mother disliked much of her taste in clothing, with only the rarest of exceptions. Anne liked bright orange and yellow dresses because they reminded her of Mischief, very vibrant blues and greens and even occasionally bright pinks. It wasn't likely that Elizabeth had any dresses that Anne felt would properly suit her. But if it satisfied her mother, she would try, anyway.

The viscountess rounded up her younger daughters, frantically arranging the preparations for their carriage to be ready. Charlotte grabbed onto Anne's arm, grinning like a child at Christmastide.

"Oh, Sister, this is so exciting," she said. "Mother was right, you know. He did appear to be utterly taken with you earlier. It's as though you found your way out of normal life and right into something from a storybook."

Anne gave her sister a smile, but she said nothing. She needed to confide in Charlotte. But right then wasn't the time. Their mother was too close and might overhear. Charlotte's idea was charming, and it was something Anne hoped her sister would find for herself as a result of her fake courtship with the duke. But for Anne, any such illusion was just that: an illusion. And that was just the way she liked it. Wasn't it?

***

"Oh, Sister, that will make you look far too pale," Elizabeth muttered, holding up a nice, pale blue dress to Anne's face as though Anne had been the one to suggest it. As she had suspected, her mother was only acknowledging the pale, light, softer colors of Elizabeth's, which was most of the dresses she had ever owned. And worse still, Elizabeth had nothing flattering to say about any of the ones she did have. Except, of course, Anne's least favorite ones.

The viscountess nodded in agreement with her eldest daughter, frowning.

"You're right," she said. "She needs something paler. Especially with her eyes so... prominent."

Anne stifled the urge to roll her eyes. It was as if her mother could never truly be proud of, or confident in, her middle daughter. Truthfully, it was a wonder that anyone in the ton believed that the Duke of Calder was interested in her.

That thought allowed doubt and worry to creep into Anne's mind as she wondered what might happen if the ton were to discover their secret. Would they be ostracized? Would they be forced into going through with marriage to maintain their status and to keep from being disowned by their families? Her breath caught in her throat, and she yearned for a moment of solitude to collect her thoughts.

"Mother," she said, giving her mother the sweetest smile she could muster. "I'm feeling a bit dizzy. Might I go out onto the balcony, just to get a little air?"

She expected a scowl or a bitter admonishment. However, her mother gave her an indulgent smile, stroking her cheek.

"Of course, darling," she said with a kindness that Anne had only heard directed at Charlotte in recent years. "I can imagine that all this sudden attention from a duke is very overwhelming for a young lady like you. But don't dally too long. We must have your dress this evening so that you can get to bed early and be well rested for tomorrow."

Anne forced herself not to flinch at her mother's backhanded compliment. She just continued to smile, softly excusing herself from the room to step out on the balcony of her elder sister's bedroom chambers. She let the fresh air fill her lungs, the cool breeze ruffling her hair and soothing her anxiety. For that moment, at least, she felt free from the societal standards and expectations to which she was always otherwise shackled. She knew she would never fit in with the proper, dry and snobby people of London's high society. She wished for a day when she wouldn't have to. Nothing was more important to her than being as free as she felt right then. But would that time ever come? Could she ever truly be herself?

When she returned inside, it was with great reluctance. It was also to the sight of her mother holding up two pink gowns, as though she herself intended to choose between the two. Anne was stricken with a sudden desire to reclaim control. She might have her mother dictating her social and romantic life. But she would not have the viscountess tell her what she could and couldn't. Not anymore.

Glancing around the room, her eyes were finally drawn to a bright orange gown that had clearly been hidden by all the other ones. It was striking, its vibrant color reminding her of Mischief's brilliant eyes and its busy swirled design reflecting both the freedom she had felt outside and the chaos she felt when having to try to conform. To Anne, it was the most beautiful dress she'd ever seen, and in one of her favourite colors. With resolve, she turned to her mother and Elizabeth with a determined smile.

"This one," she said. "This one is my choice."

As always, she expected resistance and a lecture. Bright orange was, after all, considered a gaudy color with ton society. But she was prepared to point out that it belonged to Elizabeth, not to her. And if it was all right for Elizabeth to own such a dress, then it should be acceptable for Anne to wear it.

But in a display of compliance and understanding that Anne was beginning to become familiar with, her mother shared a look with Elizabeth as the two of them nodded.

"I bought that dress for a special tea party," she said. "But Donna canceled as she was ill. I do find that dress rather vibrant and cheery."

The viscountess nodded, as if she had never had anything negative to say about Anne making such selections for herself.

"I agree, darling," she said. "I believe Anne will look very lovely in this dress."

Anne smiled, feeling as though she had won a small victory. Even if it was only because of the Duke that she was beginning to earn more respect and consideration from her family, she would enjoy it while it lasted.

That evening, back in the sanctuary of her bedchambers, Anne gazed at the selected gown, shimmering under the soft glow of candlelight. It maintained its appeal with her, so much so that she wished she had had the opportunity to purchase such a dress for herself. She supposed that Elizabeth's husband was more lenient on her than their parents were on Anne. She sighed wistfully, thinking about how much more freedom Elizabeth must have been allowed.

But as beautiful and freeing as the dress was, the weight of the farce it represented was heavy on Anne. There was much to concern her about what the Duke and she were doing. And there was also the way she felt when she was around him. He was more handsome than any man with whom she had ever interacted within the ton. And he was far more charming and witty. She knew what they had was fake. But she couldn't stop thinking about how part of her wished that it wasn't. And then, there was how her family didn't think she deserved someone like a duke. She thought the two of them got along perfectly well. But what if he could barely tolerate her, like her own family?

Just as the overwhelming emotions threatened to consume her, Mischief leaped onto the bed. He nudged her with his head, kneading her stomach with clawless paws as she nuzzled her nose against his whiskers. She giggled as the long strands tickled her face. Once he was satisfied that her mood had improved, he settled into bed beside her, purring contentedly. The rhythm of his purrs provided a comfort that words could not express.

Anne smiled softly and pulled Mischief closer, her heart finding solace in their shared moment. As they prepared for sleep, the weight of societal expectations seemed a little lighter. At least for that moment.

Chapter Sixteen

The following morning, Richard entered the drawing room with a heart strangely lighter than it had been in ages. He had been reluctant to invite Miss Huxley to promenade hour with him. But as soon as he saw how lovely she looked disheveled after a clear disagreement with her family, and he heard how beautifully she played the pianoforte, he had found himself thrilled that he had the opportunity.

He had truly never heard better pianoforte playing in all of London, not unless it was at a performance with professional musicians. And even many such professionals paled in comparison to Miss Huxley's talent.

When he entered the drawing room for breakfast, he found his mother already there. He smiled and bowed to her, but he noticed when she didn't acknowledge his entry that she was deeply engrossed in a letter she was holding. He shook his head, quietly taking his seat, glad for the chance to stay in his thoughts a little longer.

He had dressed in his finest, dark orange suit. It was one that his mother wasn't particularly fond of. But he thought the color orange was a nice color. It reminded him of sunrises and sunsets. And of Miss Huxley's mischievous Mischief. And it had embroidery that reminded Richard of waves on the ocean. It was, in fact, one of his favorite suits. And only a little of the reason was because his mother disliked it.

"Richard," his mother said, finally pulling him from the comfort of his thoughts.

He looked at the dowager duchess with a pleasant smile.

"Yes, Mother?" he asked.

She looked up at him over the top of the letter, a small smile playing on her lips.

"I just wanted to let you know that we will be joining the Westbrook's for dinner this evening," she said, sounding rather pleased with herself.

Richard's jaw clenched involuntarily, and his eyes narrowed. He supposed he should have expected this particular conversation. Unfortunately for the dowager, she would not have her way this time.

"Mother," he said, his tone courteous but firm. "You must have forgotten that I already committed to accompanying Anne and Susan to the promenade this evening. Per Susan's request, of course." He bit his tongue, choosing not to add anything about his plans with Miss Huxley right then. He knew it was a conversation he would eventually need to have. But he wanted to keep his mood as pleasant as possible for the day.

His mother's discontent was palpable as she scrutinized her son. Her sharp gaze bore into him, her lips pressed into a thin line.

"Richard," she said, her voice lowering as though the ton might hear their conversation from the privacy of their own home. "I do wonder at your recent actions. It seems like you think very little of the efforts that Lady Eleanor has been making to capture your attention."

Richard refused to respond about his obvious contempt for the young lady. Instead, he simply smiled at his mother.

"I will be sure to attend dinner with them," he said.

His mother gave him a dubious look, her nose wrinkling as though she had just smelled something terrible.

"See to it that you do," she said. You know the significance of this dinner. Our family's reputation is at stake."

Before Richard could offer a retort, his mother rose and sashayed out of the room, leaving him with the lingering air of her cold distaste. He exhaled slowly, his shoulders tense. Why could she not understand how little he wanted to do with Lady Eleanor?

When Susan entered the room, her footsteps were so light that he didn't notice her until he looked up. She had a warm smile, and she embraced Richard as she kissed his cheek.

"Where's Mother?" she asked, keeping her voice low.

Richard snorted, glancing toward the open doorway.

"Off being disappointed in me, naturally," he said dryly.

Susan gave him a sympathetic look and a nod.

"I know she is hard on you," she said. "Which is why I wanted to make sure to thank you for going along with this charade. It's for Anne, naturally. But it's just as much out of concern for you. I hold an ample affection for both of you, and it pains me deeply to witness the detrimental actions of our respective families towards you. Nevertheless, I extend my profound gratitude, dear Brother. You truly are a good man."

Richard nodded, giving his sister a wan smile.

"I wonder if that's true," he said. "However, Miss Huxley is hardly the worst company in London." *In fact, I think she might be some of the best company,* he added silently and unbiddenly.

Susan gave him a wink, her smile turning a bit mischievous.

"Are you ready, Brother?" she asked.

Richard looked at the clock, noticing that a whole hour had already passed since he awoke. He rose from his seat, offering his sister his arm and grinning.

"Let's go retrieve Miss Huxley," he said.

***

Another half hour later, Richard and Susan found themselves standing in the elegant hallway of Anne's residence. The grandeur of the home was undeniable, even for a small townhouse belonging to that of a viscount and his family. It had a warm feel to him, with the warm but inviting colors and beautiful fresh flowers in every corner of every hallway and room that he could see.

The butler led them to the grand hall to wait for Miss Huxley. It, too, seemed very welcoming, and though the townhouse was far smaller than his own family's mansion, it appeared to be far more spacious. It was truly a lovely home, something he hadn't noticed in his previous visit. It occurred to him that he never spent much time in the homes of people of lower status. Not out of any sense of snobbish ideals. He had simply not had many friends of lower stations, apart from Thomas. In truth, he had not had many friends at all.

As they waited for Miss Huxley, Richard's ears perked up at a familiar meow. With delight, he looked down to see Mischief trotting up to him with his bright orange eyes. The cat stopped at his feet, sniffing him and issuing another soft meow before affectionately nuzzling his leg. A rare chuckle escaped his lips, surprising even himself. He reached down to scratch the feline, immediately feeling the animal purr under his fingertips.

When he righted himself, Susan was looking at him with wide, inquisitive eyes.

"Excuse me, Your Grace," she teased with a grin. "But in all my life, I never knew you to be a cat person."

Richard blushed, giving his sister a playful glower. But before he could deliver a witty retort, his breath was stolen from his lungs.

Anne Huxley descended the stairs wearing a dress of the prettiest shade of orange that Richard had ever seen. It had very intricate swirling patterns that would not look out of place next to the embroidery on his own suit. If someone didn't know better, they would think that the two of them had planned matching outfits. And he didn't mind that idea at all.

The way her auburn hair shimmered, seemingly highlighted by the orange in the dress, was like the heavens themselves were sending down special rays of sunshine to make it shine. He didn't realize he had forgotten to breathe until his chest began to ache. Was she more beautiful than she had been the previous day? Or was he just seeing her for the first time?

Richard was momentarily spellbound, unable to tear his gaze away from her. He took a step forward, his heart pounding, and in a move that surprised even him, he delicately kissed Anne's gloved hand. Surprise flickered in Anne's eyes, but she allowed the intimate gesture to extend for a few heartbeats, a silent connection passing between them.

The moment was broken, to Richard's chagrin, by Miss Huxley's mother appearing, with her daughter's lady's maid, at the foot of the staircase. She dipped into an unnecessarily deep and formal curtsey, giving him a broad smile.

"Good morning, Your Grace," she said, her voice dripping with all the honey in all of England. "And to you, as well, Lady Susan."

Susan returned the curtsey and greeting. Richard reluctantly pulled his gaze off of Miss Huxley to bow to her mother. It was clear that she was determined to do everything to leave a favorable impression on Richard. In truth, he cared very little about Viscountess Huxley. He was still captivated with her middle daughter, and he was anxious for the morning ahead.

"And good morning to you, as well, Lady Huxley," Richard said, trying to give the viscountess the validation she clearly so desperately sought. Then, he turned to Miss Huxley, offering her one arm and his sister the other. "Are you ready?"

Miss Huxley blushed, her green eyes sparkling with merriment and something else he couldn't quite identify.

"Yes, Your Grace, I am," she said, taking his arm as gently as a butterfly would graze an ungloved hand.

Richard grinned at her, trying to compose himself as he led the women, lady's maid and all, out to the waiting carriage.

The atmosphere inside the carriage was alive with jovial chatter. It was such a change from his normal heavy, brooding mood that it was astonishing to Richard at first. But it didn't take him long to relax and start smiling, especially as the lady's maid was lovingly fussing about Mischief tearing a thread in her apron earlier that morning.

Miss Huxley giggled, patting her lady's maid on her hand.

"Oh, Martha, I apologise," she said. "If you'd like, I'll mend it for you. It is solely my kitten's doing, thus my responsibility. It's the least I could do."

Martha shook her head, giving her mistress a doting smile.

"I already mended it," she said, gesturing the seemingly immaculate apron. "I would never bother you with it. And he is a darling little boy. Even if he does get into trouble sometimes."

Miss Huxley laughed again, and Richard shivered with delight. Had he ever heard a sound so addictive in his life? It was practically magical.

"Oh, goodness," Susan gasped when the two women had finished talking. "I nearly forgot to mention this. I will be having my birthday celebration at Vauxhall Gardens this weekend. I do hope you will be able to come."

Miss Huxley brightened like the morning sky as she smiled and nodded eagerly.

"Oh, of course," she said. "I wouldn't miss your birthday for the world. And I just adore the merry-go-round there."

Susan grinned, nodding along with her friend.

"And isn't the food they have there just delightful?" she asked.

Miss Huxley nodded, clasping her hands together.

"There are no finer sweets in all of London, I'm sure," she said.

Richard didn't chime in on the discussion. He was content to listen to the women talk with such animation. It gave him a chance to keep stealing glances at Miss Huxley. The more she spoke, the more he wanted to hear her speak. And the more he wanted to hear her speak, the more he marveled at the effect she was having on him.

Internally, he constantly reminded himself of the true nature of their relationship. This was all an elaborate ruse, a facade to keep them both out of horrible marriages. Wasn't it?

Chapter Seventeen

"Anne, you look positively ravishing," Susan gushed as the carriage rolled along.

Anne blushed, noticing that the duke had nodded along with his sister's proclamation with a tiny smile on his face. She had noticed he kept stealing glances at her, but she was sure it was because of the color of her dress. Anne knew it had been a bold choice, one in which she had been confident at the time. But now that she was sitting in front of Richard, she began to question herself.

"It reminds me a little of Mischief," Richard said with a little chuckle.

Anne looked at him with wide eyes. That was the very reason why it was her favorite color. Had the duke come to that conclusion on his own? She glanced at Susan, who was looking at her with genuine innocence and delight. She looked back at the duke, blushing as she smiled.

"That's why it is one of my favourite colours," she said softly. She saw no reason to keep up any pretense with him. He was her best friend's brother, so there was likely a great deal he already knew about her. Besides, she wasn't truly courting him. Thus, there was no need to truly work to impress him. Not that she would, even if there was.

The Duke's eyes were soft and warm as his smile widened.

"It is very flattering on you, Miss Huxley," he said.

Anne looked him over, noting the similar color of his suit.

"Is it your favourite colour, too?" she asked. Her mother would have been mortified at her directness. But the duke merely laughed heartily, shaking his head.

"No," he said. "Although I do find it to be an attractive colour, I was fully aware that this attire would irk my mother to no end. And as it happens, I'm glad I made this choice all around now."

Anne couldn't help but laugh at the joke about irritating his mother. She understood how he felt. She often irritated her mother without meaning to. The times when she could do it intentionally brought her tiny slivers of happiness in an otherwise unbearable familial situation.

"Well, it looks dashing on you, as well," she said.

The duke grinned.

"We will make quite the pair, won't we?" he asked.

Anne blushed, but her smile grew bigger.

"I should think we will," she said. It was only after she spoke that she thought about the rest of what he'd said. Why was he now glad all around that he had chosen that suit? Was it because he knew they would stir up more whispers? Or was there something more behind his smile and compliments?

As the carriage rolled to a stop outside Hyde Park, Richard disembarked from the carriage first. He helped Susan down, then Martha, and lastly, Anne. He smiled at her as her feet touched the ground. He offered her his arm, which she took with timid excitement. The butterflies fluttered with exhilaration in her abdomen, and she couldn't help a little shiver of nervous delight.

Anne and Richard took the lead, while Susan struck up a jovial conversation with Martha a few paces behind them. Anne realized that her friend was treating the outing as though it was an official outing of courtship. She didn't know whether to be pleased or afraid. But the duke's warm, cheerful grin helped her feel a bit more at ease.

"Shall we head to Rotten Row?" Richard asked.

Anne gave him a tense smile and nodded. She knew that was where most of the higher status nobility of the ton tended to take their strolls. Would they encounter worse jeering and snide remarks there? She didn't care what anyone thought about her. She just didn't want to make the Duke regret agreeing to be seen with her.

"That sounds lovely," she lied.

As they turned south and headed toward the popular walking and riding path, Anne noticed that her fears were largely unfounded. While there was the occasional sneer or horrified glance her way, people were instantly corrected with little more than a mere nod from the Duke. Most of the noble men and women they encountered stopped to bow and curtsey, respectively, and everyone who spoke to him was polite and pleasant.

Anne noticed that no one directly addressed her. But that was fine with her. She was happy to remain shadowed by the duke. The respect he commanded from the other people in the park helped her feel less nervous and filled her with awe. For the first time in as long as she could remember, she felt safe and comfortable being out in public.

Even though no one spoke to her, she kept a small, polite smile on her face, keeping her eyes from locking with those of anyone in particular. She was determined to be on her best behavior, but not because that was what her mother wished. It was because she didn't want to cause a scene or create any reason for gossip with her dear friend and a kind soul such as the duke in her company.

"I do hope I'm not being too forward," the duke suddenly said as they turned onto Rotten Row. "But I haven't been able to stop thinking about your performance at the pianoforte yesterday. It is clear that you have a deep passion for music. I was just wondering, who is your favourite composer?"

Anne blushed. She herself had nearly forgotten about playing for him the day before. She certainly hadn't expected him to take an interest in anything she cared about. But so far that day, he had mentioned Mischief all on his own and was now inquiring about her love for music. Was he just being nice? Or did he really wish to get to know her?

"I'm rather fond of Mozart," she said softly. "I enjoy his operas most of all. Though there is something to be said for his symphonies, as well."

The Duke's eyes widened, and he looked momentarily shocked. Then, his smile returned, bigger than before.

"Mozart is my favourite composer, as well," he said with awe. "And I must agree with you. His music is glorious. I dare say it is akin to a magical experience to hear it performed." He paused, then furrowed his brow. "You like the opera, then?"

Anne nodded. It had been years since she had gotten to attend the opera. Her mother didn't see her behavior as suitable for such events.

"I do," she said. "Mozart's are the best. But I enjoy any performance where the music is delightful."

The duke nodded.

"I enjoy a good opera performance, myself," he said. "Many of the ton's fine citizens seem to only appreciate on the level at which they feel expected to enjoy it. Most people appear to just suffer through it. But I find it invigorating to attend a spirited opera."

Anne nodded, surprised at the connection she felt with Richard. It went far beyond their present arrangement. In fact, it was unlike anything she had ever experienced.

"I feel the same," she said. "It's a pity, too. The people on the stage have a true passion for their work. They deserve to be appraised for their talent. Just as phenomenal composers deserve to be appreciated for everything they are."

The duke nodded, thoughtfully, his gaze drifting for a moment. Then, he looked at her again with a hint of eagerness in his eyes.

"Would you like to accompany me to the opera tomorrow night?" he asked. "I have my own private box. And, of course, your maid is invited along to act as your chaperone."

Anne's breath caught. She knew instinctually that the invitation was impromptu. It wasn't part of his plan to ask her out again so soon. And the thought of sitting beside him in the dim ambiance of the theater, surrounded by the musical trills and crescendos that brought her joy made her heart race wildly. Martha and Susan still chatted away behind them, but in her excitement, she barely noticed them.

"I would be thrilled," she said most truthfully.

Anne felt as though she was on top of the world. The walk had been more wonderful than Anne could have dreamed, even if she were a normal ton lady. And now, the duke, who made her feel perfectly at ease at all times, wished for her to join him at the opera, which was a great love of hers. She thought nothing could tear down her delighted mood.

Yet, as they rounded a corner, a familiar and utterly unwelcome face came into view. Sebastian, accompanied by Lady Beatrice noticed their group at the same time Anne noticed them.

A smug expression spread across his face, and Anne realized with horror that he was encircled by a group of notorious gossipmongers. The very group with which Lady Beatrice always surrounded herself. The tension in the air was palpable. Anxiety flooded Anne, and she desperately wished she could turn on her heel and flee. But Richard and Susan noticed them, as well, and Susan moved to stand between the duke and Anne.

Sebastian opened his mouth, undoubtedly, to say something atrocious. But Richard stepped forward, dipping into a deep, slow bow.

"Good day," he said. His greeting was pleasant enough, but his voice carried the faintest undercurrents of icy warning that could be easily missed if a person didn't know him very well.

Clearly, Sebastian and Lady Beatrice noticed. They shared a taken aback glance before bowing and curtseying, respectively, in return. The two groups spent a moment exchanging awkward, tense pleasantries and forced smiles. But with the Duke's formidable status and no-nonsense demeanor, none of them dared to slight Anne. Even so, Anne was glad when the larger group bade them farewell and carried on down the path.

Richard offered her his arm again, giving her a mischievous smile.

"Are you ready to continue, Miss Huxley?" he asked.

Anne gave him a grateful smile as she took his arm.

"I am," she said.

***

Later that afternoon, Anne returned home, bidding her companions farewell with a warm embrace to her dear friend and a polite curtsey to the duke. It wasn't yet time for dinner, and it appeared that the rest of her family was resting in their respective chambers. She felt obliged, as she did not feel disposed to conversing with any of them at present.

She made her way up the stairs, wrestling with the heaviness of the day's events. It had been largely pleasant, apart from the tension of the encounter with Sebastian and Lady Beatrice. But that single event had been enough to remind Anne that the entire ton was watching the duke and her. More specifically, they were looking for anything rumor-worthy or gossip inducing. It made her as frustrated as it did nervous, and despite the lively conversation she'd had with the Duke, she felt drained and stressed.

It wasn't that she didn't enjoy herself when she was with the duke. In fact, quite the opposite was true. Her time with Richard provided her first real connection with someone apart from Charlotte and Susan. She didn't even feel as connected to her parents as she felt with the duke, as strange as that notion was. With him, she felt that she could be her true self. It seemed as though the duke appreciated who she was.

But what if she was wrong? What if he was simply tolerating her spirited attitude and lacking decorum for the sake of Susan, and for the ruse they were trying to pull? It was disappointing that the relationship they seemed to be forming was happening in the center of such a big deception. It was hard to know for sure if any of it was truly real, or if it was all part of an act. Anne didn't want to think such a thing, not of a man who was as kind and protective as the duke. But what else could she possibly expect from such an arrangement?

As Anne entered her bedchamber, her footsteps echoed softly on the polished wooden floor. She closed the door softly behind her to not disturb anyone who might be resting. Then, with a sigh, she sank into her plush armchair, her fingers absently stroking the soft fabric of her gown.

A soft mew drew her attention over to her bed. There, she saw Mischief, who had apparently been napping and had just noticed her return. He rose up, practically standing on his toes as he arched his back in a big stretch. He then did the stretch that always made Anne giggle, taking a couple of steps forward, then dragged his back legs as he stretched once more. Finally, he hopped down off the bed, promptly making his way over to his mistress and jumping into her lap.

Stroking his soft fur, Anne allowed herself to immerse in her thoughts, finding solace in her cat's company. Mischief's presence was the only true respite Anne ever got from the intricacies of society and the expectations and eyes that were on her at all times. When she sat petting the loving, sweet animal, none of the stresses of the world could get to her. The animal which had incidentally become her biggest source of love and comfort reminded her that no matter how chaotic and stressful life got, there were anchors to keep her steady.

Chapter Eighteen

By the time Richard and Susan took Miss Huxley home from their stroll in the park, they had two hours before the dinner with the Westbrooks was to begin. Susan looked just as displeased as Richard felt as she sighed and sank back against the coach seat.

"I wish those two would suddenly become indisposed with a fit of megrim," she muttered.

Richard chuckled, nodding.

"I agree, Sister," he said. "Though I firmly believe that, even if they were at the brink of departing from this world, they would insist on presiding over this splendid dinner."

Susan rolled her eyes. Then, her face broke out into a grin.

"Perhaps," she said. "But before long, she and all the simpletons akin shall depart, relinquishing their presence and heed. Anne and you seem to be getting on just like a true courting couple. I dare say, there isn't a soul amongst the ton who remains unconvinced of your courtship."

Richard smiled and nodded, but his heart raced wildly. He couldn't explain it, but he had felt compelled to ask Miss Huxley to the opera the following day. Not out of obligation or duty. But something in him had expelled the words from his lips, even before they had fully formed in his mind. And as soon as he had, he had been thrilled endlessly when she had accepted his invitation. Something about her was refreshing and enticing, and every minute he spent with her felt like a blessing. Fake courtship or not, he knew he would have a wonderful time the following night.

His mother was expectedly bitter when they returned. She directed Susan upstairs to refresh herself, seizing Richard by the arm.

"You try my patience," she hissed.

Richard blinked at her, taken aback. His mother had never been particularly affectionate. But one would think he had just skipped the dinner altogether, rather than returning home in just enough time to attend it. He pulled away from his mother, shaking his head.

"I told you that I would make it, and I have," he said. "I beseech you to cease your efforts henceforth."

With that, he stalked off to his chambers. He decided immediately that he would not change for the Westbrooks. Instead, he washed and re-combed his hair, reapplying some cologne. Then, he paced the floor for the next hour, until he had to go back downstairs to escort his mother and sister to the waiting carriage.

When they arrived at the home of Lady Victoria and Lady Eleanor, Richard alighted from the carriage onto the cobbled driveway of the Westbrook estate. The mansion and grounds were grand, that much was clear. But to Richard, it was exactly the same as every insipid, shallow ton member he had ever encountered.

His eyes followed the figures of the dowager and Susan as they proceeded into the mansion, their silhouettes shimmering in the soft glow of lanterns. Unsurprisingly, his mother's attitude immediately changed as they knocked on the door, becoming a sickening sweet that Richard had come to associate with her fake efforts to make others think they were a perfect, loving family.

They were greeted at the entrance by Lord and Lady Westbrook, who exchanged warm pleasantries with his mother. Richard bowed and muttered the customary greetings and gratitude for the dinner invitation, even though he would have preferred to thank them for not inviting him to anything, ever. None to his surprise, Lady Eleanor was standing behind her mother coyly, her poised demeanor barely masking her eagerness as she batted her eyelashes at Richard.

"I'm so glad you made it, Your Grace," she said, her tone affecting a honey-like innocence.

Richard's stomach churned as he bowed.

"Good evening, Lady Eleanor," he said blandly.

Lady Victoria shot Richard a calculating look that did not escape his notice. He was aware that the woman had every intention of seeing her daughter married to him. His only reprieve was Susan's coolness to Lady Eleanor and his knowledge that no such match would ever be made between him and the young lady before him.

When they reached the drawing room, servants stood along the walls, waiting to serve glasses of wine and champagne. Richard took some wine gratefully, handing a glass to his sister. They toasted silently, sharing a secret look of understanding about the futility of the current dinner party. But predictably, Lady Victoria had no intention of allowing Richard to go unnoticed for very long.

"I do hope you intend to attend the upcoming Season balls," she said, batting her eyes flirtatiously at him. "I should think that an escort as charming and prestigious as a duke would do a young lady's reputation a world of good. Especially a young lady as sweet and delicate as my dear Eleanor."

Richard stiffened. It wasn't out of character for Lady Victoria to be bold with her thoughts and desires. But he wasn't going to take the bait. He had been laying the workings to show all of London that he was courting Miss Huxley. He could hardly announce such news at a dinner that was clearly so important to his mother. But nor was he going to humor Lady Victoria by affirming her request.

Susan, ever diligent, came to his rescue. She reached over, patting his hand gently and giving Lady Eleanor a pointed look, carefully avoiding the gaze of both their mothers.

"I meant to tell you that Anne said she had a wonderful time today," she said. Her voice was sweet, and her eyes were innocent as she smiled at Richard. But beneath the innocence shone a sparkle of impish glee. She was not having any more of their host's pressure than Richard was. He gave her a smirk and nodded.

"As did I, Sister," she said. "I dare say that I enjoyed our stroll today more than I've enjoyed the park in some time."

Lady Eleanor blanched, wrinkling her nose at the mention of Miss Huxley's name. But her mother would not be deterred. She widened her smile, her eyes dark with intensity and determination.

"Promenade hour at the park is an event, indeed," she said. "My Eleanor loves taking a stroll along Rotten Row. It's given her skin the lovely glow it has now, finding her customary dose of sunshine there."

Richard nodded, smiling politely, but silently, at Lady Eleanor. He didn't notice any glow, except the shine of sheer eagerness in the young lady's blue eyes. In fact, she appeared to be a bit too pale, bordering on looking like an artist had colored her in with solid white paint. To him, she was not traditionally pretty. But then, his judgment was affected by her temperament and attitude. Perhaps, she was quite lovely. But she made Richard's stomach churn.

Richard realized they had been there for nearly an hour and no dinner announcement had been made. He looked at the clock, noting that it was nearly seven o'clock. He glanced questioningly at his mother, who refused to meet his gaze as she engaged in conversation with Lady Victoria. But then, their hostess turned to the musicians in the room, motioning for them to start playing. They warmed up their instruments, and Richard's heart dropped when he heard the first strains of a waltz playing. Surely, Lady Victoria didn't intend for her small handful of guests to dance.

His suspicions were confirmed when Lady Victoria gave him an expectant look.

"Eleanor loves dancing," she said, not bothering to conceal her intent as she spoke. "And the waltz happens to be her favourite. I thought tonight might be a good chance for her to get to practice it a little."

Richard sighed heavily, also not bothering to hide his resentment for the situation. Naturally, Lady Victoria didn't seem fazed by his irritation. Everyone in the room, apart from Susan, was staring at him intently. He didn't need to guess what was expected of him. He was going to have to ask Lady Eleanor to dance.

Stiffly, he rose, glowering at his mother who pretended not to notice. He offered a tense arm to Lady Eleanor, leaving his gesture as the only invitation he intended to offer. She didn't need words, and she had grabbed onto his arm before he had finished lifting it. She beamed at him as though he had just offered her courtship right then and let him lead her to the center of the large drawing room which, he noticed then, had been cleared of all furniture and tables. He had never been inside the Westbrook's home, but there were dents in the carpet where furniture legs and stumps had long rested, and everything was in a suspiciously perfect circle around the area where he now stood with Lady Eleanor.

Silently, he began leading the young woman in the dance. He noticed right away that she was far less graceful than Miss Huxley in the dance. The expression on her face, however, told him that she thought she was as dainty on her feet as an angel. He just managed to not roll his eyes as he went through the motions of the dance. He didn't enjoy the dance at all. All he could think about was how magical his dance with Miss Huxley had been.

His distraction became apparent when he accidentally stepped on Lady Eleanor's toes. To her credit, she didn't yelp, but she gave him an annoyed glance. He halted the dance to give her a brief, sheepish smile.

"Apologies," he mumbled, straightening himself to begin dancing again.

Lady Eleanor's expression changed immediately, back to the empty beaming look she'd had when she'd accepted the offer to dance.

"It's quite all right," she said with a giggle. "Perhaps, I will get plenty of chances to help you practice your dancing technique."

Richard uttered an awkward chuckle, but he said nothing. He remained silent throughout the rest of the dance, breathing a sigh of relief when it was over.

At last, the dinner announcement was made, and everyone filed to the dining room. Lady Eleanor was gushing to her mother about the dance, clearly not ruined for her by him stepping on her. Her mother was practically crowing with pride, smiling brightly at her daughter. The dowager duchess even gave Richard a nod of approval. Did she really not notice his displeasure?

He knew she didn't care about his recent association with Miss Huxley, or how she might feel about him dancing with another lady if their budding relationship had been real. But was she so focused on her plan to marry him off to Lady Eleanor that she truly cared so little about his happiness?

He was far from surprised to find that he was seated beside Lady Eleanor at the dinner table. Fortunately, Susan was on his other side, which offered him a marginal amount of solace. His mother immediately engaged Lady Victoria in conversation, making it a point to ignore any glances Richard shot her way. Susan gave him a brilliant smile and opened her mouth to speak. But Lady

Eleanor positioned herself in close proximity to him, approaching the border of impropriety, and batted her eyelashes at him.

"I've heard that Lord and Lady Benson are to host a grand ball this Season," she said. "And of course, you know that they are very well-renowned in the ton. A ball at their estate is sure to be the event of the season. I think we will make quite a stir by attending together."

Richard stared at her blankly. Even for her, that was especially forward. It was terribly rude and untoward for a lady to presume an invitation to anything from a gentleman until he had made mention of it himself. And he certainly had no intention of asking her to any ball, least of all one that was alleged to be such a huge event. But he didn't get the chance to answer because she began speaking again.

"And I would love to take a walk along the Thames River next week," she said. "I think that would make a lovely outing, don't you?"

Richard shook his head, fed up with Lady Eleanor's conversation, domination and her bold behavior. But she continued chattering, not allowing him or Susan to get a word in edgewise.

Suddenly, amidst the noise of clinking silverware and incessant babble from Lady Eleanor, a familiar melody drifted from the pianoforte in the corner of the room. It was the tune he'd heard Miss Huxley playing the day he had gone to her home to invite her to Promenade Hour. He was instantly transported back to that day, her disheveled appearance, the magic that had flowed from her fingers as she played like an angel and the blush in her cheeks as he'd paid her compliments. It offered him a much needed, albeit temporary, reprieve from the tension.

When his mother, his sister and he returned home, he waited for his mother to retire. Then, he slipped back out, making his way to White's. His mother had been unexpectedly placid on the way home. But his nerves were completely raw, and he couldn't stand the thought of being confined to the walls of his family's home.

A broad smile broke out onto his face when he entered the club. There, at their favorite table, sat Thomas, looking toward the door as though he had been expecting Richard. Richard made his way to his friend, placing his drink order and exchanging greetings with his friend. As he waited for his drink, he couldn't help thinking about how drastically different his genuine, delightful interactions with Miss Huxley were compared to the societal norm exemplification displayed by the Westbrook's.

He had been raised to behave properly and with perfect decorum his entire life. And yet, he found it so tedious and painful that he wanted nothing more than to escape it. Unfortunately, as duke, he would never have such luck. But Miss Huxley provided refreshing relief from those pressures. He truly enjoyed her company and her unorthodox mannerisms and spirited nature. He wished that he could be more like her.

Seemingly noticing Richard's contemplative mood, Thomas arched an eyebrow and leaned in.

"Pray, where do you wander Richard?" he inquired.

Richard sighed and ran a hand through his hair.

"It seems that I am growing rather fond of Miss Huxley,

He said, feeling the words for the very first time as they left his lips. "It was all supposed to be a façade. But the more time I spend in her company, the more I discern that I may freely express my true self and need not constantly bear the weight of impeccable conduct."

Thomas looked at him thoughtfully for a moment as he sipped his drink.

"If there are genuine feelings between you two, perhaps, the courtship doesn't have to remain a charade," he said.

Richard stared at Thomas, ready to object. But he thought about what his friend had just said. Was Thomas right? Was there a chance that he could cease the charade with Miss Huxley and pursue a real courtship?

Chapter Nineteen

"You're going where?" Charlotte burst into Anne's room the next afternoon as she was mulling over her dresses.

Anne turned around, laughing as she turned just in time for Charlotte to leap into her arms. She had spent the previous evening with a friend of hers who was married and preparing for the arrival of her first child. She hadn't been home when Anne had told her parents of her plans to attend the opera with the duke. But clearly, they had informed her as soon as she returned home.

"The Duke has invited me to attend the opera with him tonight," she said.

Charlotte squealed with delight, clapping her hands excitedly as her curls bounced.

"This is so exciting," she said, taking Anne's hands and swinging them. "I just know that you will soon be the duchess of Calder."

Anne's smile wilted, and she guided her sister away from the open wardrobe and over to the bed. She sat her down, giving her a wan look.

"Charlotte," she said, keeping her voice low. "I'm not truly courting the Duke. It's just pretend. But I need you to not speak a word of it to anyone."

Charlotte frowned, clearly confused.

"I won't, Sister," she said. "But why would you two pretend to be courting?"

Anne took a deep breath and quietly explained the situation. When she was finished, however, Charlotte was grinning impishly.

"That is a clever idea," she said. "However, I do not believe that what is happening between the two of you is pretend."

It was Anne's turn to frown. She looked at her sister with confusion.

"What do you mean?" she asked.

Charlotte winked at her sister.

"How many gentlemen do you know would invite a lady to the opera for their second official outing if he wasn't interested in her?" she asked.

Anne opened her mouth to answer before realizing that she could not. She stared at her sister, who shrugged, patting her hands gently.

"Just allow whatever happens to happen," she said. "It is a brilliant idea to keep everyone from forcing you into horrible marriages. Verily, I declare to you, the gaze of his eyes when they rest upon you do not resemble that of a gentleman engaged in mere fiction."

Anne nodded, her cheeks warming. She was aware that he was warm, kind and delightful, and that there was definitely a great deal of common ground between them. But she could never allow herself to believe that he would ever truly take a romantic interest in her. It felt good to tell Charlotte her secret, though, and she embraced her sister.

"Perhaps," she said, despite her rising doubt. "For now, however, I need help choosing a dress for tonight. I want to look my best."

Charlotte giggled, covering her mouth as she rose and walked over to the wardrobe.

"You didn't say that you needed to," she said. "That is quite revealing, indeed, Sister."

Anne's blush deepened, and she joined her younger sister, giving her a playful nudge.

"Please, just help me, you wicked thing," she said, joining her sister in her laughter.

Within an hour, Anne had selected a green silk gown that was embroidered with white pearls and adorned with lace ribbons, adding to it her matching gloves and shoes. It was a notably more subdued color than the orange one she had worn the day before, but she selected it by design. She might enjoy watching her mother squirm with her vibrant clothing choices. But she wanted to look as though she belonged beside the duke and not leave him wishing he'd never asked her to the opera.

Charlotte left to go and prepare to dine with her parents, and Martha came to help Anne dress. The green dress's bodice was

135

perfectly fitted to her form, while its empire waisted skirt billowed around her legs like a visible green breeze. She opted for a laurel wreath to rest atop her head after Martha styled her curly hair with half of it rolled into a neat bun and the lower half pinned around her head on each side, with one final tuft of curls dangling down past her shoulders. It was her compromise to her modest, toned-down outfit.

Each brush stroke and dress adjustment felt momentous to Anne as Martha added dashes of rouge and rosewater perfume with a flourish. She thought about what Charlotte had said, trying to recall the way in which the duke looked at her. She could see the genuine friendliness in his eyes when he smiled at her. Did she perchance observe him ogling at her with a slight gape on the previous day? And was he really stealing glances at her when he thought she wasn't looking, or had she imagined it all?

Mischief suddenly darted under her dress, passing quickly between her feet as he chased a particle of floating dust. She giggled, pausing to pat him and soothe her fragile nerves.

"You must behave tonight, my darling, she whispered to the feline, who merely purred in response, seemingly indifferent to her admonition.

Martha laughed heartily.

"One could be forgiven for thinking you were speaking to a child, if they heard these interactions before they saw them," she said fondly.

Anne smiled and nodded, giving the animal a doting kiss on the head before standing upright again.

"He is my child," she said. "He just happens to have fur and speak a different language."

The two women laughed.

When she was ready at last, Charlotte took her leave and Martha escorted Anne down the stairs, prepared to act as her chaperone for the evening. They walked together to the parlor, where Anne could hear her parents talking animatedly. The Duke must have already arrived. Suddenly, she was filled with excitement, and she had to force herself to remain calm as she stepped into the room.

Her parents were conversing with the Duke of Calder about some menial social gossip. But their voices faded away as Anne, entirely captivated, couldn't tear her eyes away from the duke. He looked incredibly dashing in his cream-colored suit. His dark hair was perfectly combed, save for one strand that insisted on dangling beside his left eye. His blue eyes crinkled at the corners as he laughed politely at some joke the viscount made. Her mother's diverted attention alerted him to Anne's entrance, and he looked toward the door.

Their eyes met, and the intensity in his gaze set Anne's heart and stomach aflutter. She offered a shy smile, trying to breathe through the butterflies that swirled in her stomach. The connection she previously thought she felt with him returned with amplified force, and she found it difficult to look away from him. She was enthralled with him, as though he had waved a magic wand and put her under a spell.

"Miss Huxley, you look absolutely beautiful," he said as he rose from his seat beside her father, a crooked smile spreading across his face.

Anne blushed. She might have thought he was just being polite. But his eyes were wide and sparkling, and there was no deception or polite refrain in them. He seemed truly impressed, which made her heart race faster.

"You look very handsome, Your Grace," Anne said, dipping into a curtsey.

The duke approached her, offering her his arm. Meanwhile, the viscount and viscountess also rose, following the duke to where Anne stood.

"Have a wonderful evening, darling," her mother said. Her look of appraisal was brief and approving, and she patted Anne gently on the back. The viscount gave her a nod, flashing her a brief smile.

"Mind your manners," he said. His tone was jovial, but Anne had no doubt that there was actual warning in his words.

Anne nodded, her cheeks growing hot with embarrassment. The duke caught her eye, unseen by her parents and gave her one of his classic winks.

"Shall we?" he asked, ignoring her parents and gesturing toward the door.

Anne nodded, smiling gratefully.

"Yes, let's," she said.

The carriage waited for the three of them outside, with a footman opening the door as they approached. Richard helped Martha inside the coach, then turned to help Anne. She was expecting the bolt of lightning that occurred each time the duke touched her. But it still took away her breath for a brief moment as she stepped gracefully into the carriage. Once the duke himself was aboard, the carriage pulled away from her home, rolling smoothly toward the theater.

"Do you have a particular favourite opera?" the duke asked as Anne's home faded from sight.

Anne thought it over before smiling.

"I enjoy all of Mozart's operas," she said. "But I suppose you wish to know if I have a favourite besides his?"

The duke shrugged, his lips twitching and his eyes sparkling mysteriously.

"If your favourite one is one composed by Mozart, there's no harm in that," he said. "My personal favourite is 'The Marriage of Figaro.'"

Anne grinned. She could hardly believe it, and she had to steady her breathing before she spoke again.

"That happens to be my favourite, as well," she said bashfully.

The duke grinned.

"What a coincidence," he said impishly. "Mozart truly is a master of his craft. I daresay that none deserve accolades more than he."

Anne nodded excitedly.

"He is a musical genius, to be sure," she said. "I attribute his talent and inspiration to my love for music."

Richard nodded, his smile so warm and genuine.

"I think I wouldn't have such a great love for the opera, were it not for his incomparable skills," he said.

Anne felt as though they were riding on clouds. She had never been able to discuss music or composers with anyone in such depth. Nor had she met anyone who shared her fondness for her favorite opera, or for Mozart himself. It felt too good to be true, and she discretely pinched herself to ensure that she wasn't dreaming. Even the thought of how her relationship with the duke was only pretend didn't dampen her spirits as the carriage reached town.

When they reached the theater, however, her heart sank a little. No sooner than the duke had helped her alight from the carriage did the stares and whispers begin. The duke, ever the elegant and poised gentleman, held his head high as he escorted her to his private box. He blatantly ignored everyone who gaped at them, not bothering to offer any pleasantries or expected greetings. He left several more stares in his wake by doing so. And Anne couldn't help but giggle.

The grandeur of the opera box left Anne astounded. The lavish decor, the purple plush velvet seats, and the full view of the entire stage were beyond anything she had ever imagined. It was certainly a far cry from the usual upper tier gallery seats her father purchased for their family when they attended the theater. He could have afforded better, more expensive seating. But he was always expecting Anne to make a spectacle, so he chose not to invest much in the outings. Susan and she had also attended the opera together, but they had always been in the standing area. But in the splendor of the duke's private box, all those thoughts and memories were washed away.

As Richard got himself settled in the seat beside her, the faint scent of his sandalwood cologne intensified her awareness of his presence. The subtle fragrance filled her senses, and Anne found herself unable to concentrate on anything but the proximity of the duke that the world thought she would soon be courting. *Would wish that I was,* she thought wistfully as the curtain slowly rose on the stage. She realized she meant the thought as soon as she had it. And she let herself imagine for a moment that it could really happen.

The opening scene of Figaro's and Susanna's wedding was revealed, and Anne immediately recognized the opera as 'The Marriage of Figaro'. She smiled at the duke, who gave her one of his heart-stopping winks.

"Surprise," he said.

Anne blushed, beaming at him.

"How delightful," she gushed. "Thank you so very much."

Richard pretended to bow as he sat in his seat.

"My pleasure, Miss Huxley," he said warmly.

Anne was instantly enthralled. She had seen the opera a couple of times. But she was just as enthralled with it as she had been the very first time. As the count entered the stage, professing his desire to exercise his right to the bride on her wedding night, Anne's heart squeezed. She could imagine the feeling of being forced to touch a man she didn't want. And as Figaro was reminded of his debt to Marcellina and the prospect of being married to her to pay off what he owed, Anne listened intently. Suddenly, she noticed a parallel between the opera and her own life, one which had never applied before. She was pretending to court the duke to avoid being forced into a marriage. And he was doing the same with her.

During intermission, the duke turned to Anne, his cheeks flushed from laughter at the actors' antics during the comedic scenes.

"Are you enjoying yourself?" he asked.

Anne nodded eagerly, clasping her hands together and placing them against her bosom.

"Oh, yes, Your Grace," she said, positively brimming with pleasure and joy. "These actors are truly exceptional."

Richard nodded, his grin widening.

"I believe this is the best performance I have ever seen of this play," he said. "Perhaps, the best opera performance I have ever seen altogether."

Anne nodded once again, surprised at their common remarks about the performance.

"I believe that man is the best casting for Figaro I have ever seen," she said.

The duke looked surprised, and Anne knew what he was going to say before he spoke.

"As do I," he said. "Fancy that. We seem to be very much of the same mind about the opera."

Anne blushed, giggling.

140

"Great minds think alike, I hear," she said boldly.

Richard studied her for a moment before winking at her again.

"I must agree with you, Miss Huxley," he said softly.

As they talked and pointed out the similarities to the opera and their own close calls with arranged marriages, it was easy for Anne to forget that they were not truly a couple. But every so often, she would silently chide herself and remind herself that their romance was simply for show. After all, how could something that was mere pretense truly feel so profoundly real? She couldn't let herself forget the situation. But it was so easy to get carried away.

The evening drew to a close all too soon for Anne's liking, as the final act showed the characters celebrating a joyful reconciliation and the power of love, and the curtain fell as Anne and the duke leapt from their seats, applauding wildly with the delight of the performance. As Richard escorted her home and the pair gushed about their favorite parts of the performance, Anne was filled with a mix of regret at the night's ending and the anticipation of future encounters with the duke. Was she mistaken when she thought she sensed a bit of disappointment in the duke as they reached her home, as well?

Anne's mind was overrun with thoughts of the Duke as she prepared for bed. The sandalwood cologne he wore seemed to be clinging to the insides of her nostrils, a tangible reminder of the unforgettable evening. But now that she was out of his intoxicating presence, she thought rationally about him. Was there any way the Duke could ever truly desire someone like her? Or was she allowing herself to get too attached to a man she would end up having to walk away from?

Chapter Twenty

The following morning, images from the opera lingered in Richard's mind. He lay in bed, the soft sheets enticing him to lie and bask in their comfort a little longer. The entirety of the evening prior felt surreal to him. Miss Huxley's infectious laughter seemed to have become part of his soul. The gentle touch of her hand had sent wave after wave of heat coursing through him in a way he had never experienced before.

Her rapt attention during the performance confirmed that she did, indeed, have a true love for the opera, unlike most of the flaky women in the ton who sat watching, glazed-eyed and clearly bored, merely seeking the approval of a nobleman. Her enthusiasm had been a revelation, a stark contrast to the tasteless behavior he'd been taught to expect from women with her reputation.

Yet despite the circulating rumors about her, he recognized that he genuinely relished her presence. He also realized that he didn't mind that. In fact, he was already looking forward to the next time he would get to see her. How had she never captured his attention before Susan came up with her grand plan to fool the ton with their faux courtship? She was just the breath of fresh air he had skeptically hoped for in ton women. How had he never noticed her before?

His mind reluctantly shifted to the day ahead. He knew he would be expected at breakfast with his mother and sister, the latter of whom was celebrating her twentieth birthday. The breakfast part filled him with dread. But he had procured something special for Susan, and he was excited to give it to her. Having been shopping with her recently, he knew it was something she wanted. And he delighted in bringing the sweet, thrilled smile to his younger sister's face.

Sliding out of bed, Richard called for Watson, selecting a deep navy coat and light blue cravat with matching light blue boots. He opted to not wear a hat that day. He knew it irked his mother when he didn't wear hats, as it was a fashion statement for men, particularly those of his station. He also hated hats, and only wore them when society deemed it absolutely necessary. Watson came and dressed him so quickly that Richard hardly got to finish exchanging their usual morning pleasantries. But there was one more thing he needed before he could go downstairs.

He walked over to his dresser, where his riding, traveling and fencing outfits were folded, reaching in the top drawer. He pulled out a square box the size of his palm, wrapped in silver paper and topped with a bright red bow, Susan's favorite color. He tucked it into the pocket of his coat, then headed down to join his mother and sister.

Susan was the first to acknowledge him, smiling sweetly at him as he entered the breakfast room. He approached her with a warm smile of his own, leaning in to place a gentle kiss on his sister's cheek.

"Happy birthday, dear Sister," he said, gazing fondly at his sister. It was still hard for him to believe that she was a young woman now, not the child he used to chase and play with in the gardens of Calder Estate. But he was proud of the woman she had become, and he adored her.

Susan beamed at him with a soft giggle.

"Thank you, sweet Brother," she said. "I've so been looking forward to my birthday this year."

Richard grinned and nodded. He knew how much she loved Vauxhall Gardens. And he intended to make the evening special in every single way once they arrived there. He'd already made preliminary arrangements, and everything else would be up to Susan when they arrived there.

With a dramatic flourish, he presented her with the box, holding it out to her in his open palm.

"I got you something," he said.

Susan took the box, looking at Richard affectionately.

"You didn't need to do that," she said. "You're already treating me this evening."

Richard shrugged, still smiling.

"I think that will go nicely with the evening," he said mysteriously.

Susan gave him a bemused look. Then, she unwrapped the gift, her eyes widening in delight when she revealed its contents.

Rubies sparkled in the morning light in its delicate silver setting, casting a kaleidoscope of small red beams on the skirt of her dress.

"Oh, Richard, it's the exact one I wanted," she gasped, clutching the necklace in her hand with a smile on her face and tears in her eyes.

Richard nodded, pleased to see his sister so happy. He looked at her with a mixture of pride and tenderness.

"I know," he said. "I knew how much you wanted it, and I thought there was no lady more deserving of it in all of London than you."

Susan leapt from her seat and threw her arms around Richard.

"Thank you," she repeated, pulling away and gesturing for him to help her put it on. He complied, clasping it around her neck and feeling another rush of glee as she squealed, looking down to see how it looked on her.

"I knew it would be just wonderful," she said with awe.

Richard nodded once again, noting how lovely the necklace truly was.

"You look beautiful, Sister," he said.

The moment was sweet and joyous, a temporary respite from the heaviness that had been weighing on him. But as with all good things in his life, the moment was short-lived. His mother, clearly impatiently waiting for the interaction between brother and sister to end, set aside her coffee and looked at Richard with a furrowed brow.

"Richard, the newspaper columns are positively buzzing about your appearance with Miss Huxley last night," she said. Her tone was clipped, and her eyes blazed with barely contained frustration.

Richard sighed, shrugging as he sat down beside her sister.

"Aren't they always abuzz with something?" he asked.

His mother's eyes narrowed, and she shook her head slowly.

"How you could not take things more seriously, I will never understand," she said. "I'm not sure what your intentions are with this ridiculous display, but I do hope you see reason soon."

Richard raised an eyebrow, giving his mother a firm, warning gaze.

144

"Am I doing something illegal or roguish?" he asked. "Have I been found drunk in an alley with my clothing ripped, gotten in deep with gambling sharks or jeopardized a young lady's reputation?"

His mother clenched her jaw, studying Richard for a moment before shaking her head.

"There are many other ways to induce a scandal," she said as though issuing a warning. "You'd do well to remember that."

Richard shrugged again, pretending to care about the food he was putting on his plate.

"I remember how society works, Mother," he said. "But I do not operate solely according to what society wants." There was a warning in his words, as well. He was informing his mother that he would not be dictated to by anyone, and she surely knew that included her.

The dowager duchess stared at her son for a moment, clearly wishing to say more. Eventually, however, she huffed, retrieving her coffee cup.

"Well, Lady Eleanor has been very graceful about this whole ordeal," she said. "She is very infatuated with you, it seems. Even your recent actions have done nothing to deter her. I hope you will keep that in mind, as well."

Richard froze. There was nothing graceful about Lady Eleanor, including her dancing. Not compared to Miss Huxley. But he didn't say those things. He simply looked at his sister, choosing to ignore his mother's pedantry.

"Happy birthday again, Sister," he said.

Throughout the rest of the meal, Richard remained silent. He did his best to keep his face relaxed and pleasant as Susan gushed about all the things she wanted to do at Vauxhall Gardens that evening. Their mother indulged her excitement, making casual remarks about suggestions for what she should wear. It occurred to Richard that she would likely be after Susan to marry soon. Likely the only reason she hadn't focused more on that subject so far was because she was intent on seeing Richard married to Lady Eleanor. But once that happened, or once he had sufficiently tricked everyone into thinking that he intended to marry Miss Huxley, he had no doubt that the dowager duchess would move on to marrying off Susan. Richard sighed heavily at the thought. His sister was so full of life and spirited, much like Miss Huxley herself. It saddened him to think of the pressure she would endure until she married.

As breakfast concluded, the butler entered the breakfast room with Thomas right behind him. Richard shot up from his seat, grateful for the interjection. Thomas politely greeted the dowager and gave Susan a lingering smile as he wished her a happy birthday. Then, he grinned at Richard, holding up his fencing equipment.

"Care to accept a challenge in fencing?" he asked.

Richard smiled gratefully at his friend.

"I would be delighted," he said.

Richard hurried upstairs to fetch his own equipment. Then, he met Thomas in the estate's practice room that was just off the cellar of the mansion. Thomas had already donned his gear, so Richard did the same, grinning at his friend even though he knew Thomas couldn't see his face through the mask.

"If I win, you buy the next round of drinks at White's," he said, issuing the same wager they always had with one another.

Thomas nodded, holding his foil in the ready position.

"You have yourself a deal," he said.

The men sparred and struck like practiced dancers, slashing their weapons with expert ease and sharp strikes. Richard was typically a skilled fencing opponent. But more than once, Thomas got a good jab at his jacket, straight into the protective plastron. With his usual observant eye, Thomas must have noticed the change in Richard. About twenty minutes into their match, he lowered his foil and raised his mask.

"You seem rather distracted today, Richard," he said, bemused. "Should I hazard a guess as to why?"

Richard tried to shrug off his friend's words with a carefree grin.

"I'm not sure what you mean," he lied.

Thomas chortled, shaking his head.

"As I suspected," he said. "Would Miss Huxley have anything to do with your all-consuming thoughts?"

Richard scoffed, trying to pretend the notion was ludicrous. He was trying to keep his mind off Miss Huxley for a little while. Thoughts of her were becoming overwhelming. And with her attending Susan's birthday celebration that evening, he didn't want to be out of sorts when they went to retrieve her.

"Are you just trying to avoid losing this match?" he asked, trying to change the subject.

Thomas raised an eyebrow, and he looked as though he was trying to decide whether he should pursue the issue or let it go. Eventually, he seemed to choose the latter. He lowered his mask and lifted his foil once more.

"Not in your wildest dreams, Richard," he said.

They resumed the match, which Thomas inevitably won. Richard tried to keep his focus on his friend and their little competition. But deep down, he knew that Thomas had sensed his complex feelings for Miss Huxley. He thought back to what Thomas had said about their relationship growing beyond that of a pretense. He still wasn't convinced. But the more he thought about it, the more appealing the idea was becoming.

***

Later that day, Richard dressed to join his family to journey to Vauxhall Gardens. He hadn't mentioned Miss Huxley and her family attending the celebration. But when the carriage turned onto the spot along the Thames River where the Huxley family carriage was pulling up, his mother noticed instantly.

"Is it proper to invite Miss Huxley to Susan's party?" she asked bitterly.

Richard didn't have to answer. Susan glared at their mother, giving her an indignant huff.

"Anne is my dearest friend," she said. "And her family is dear to me, as well. And it is my birthday. I will invite whomever I please."

Those words silenced the dowager duchess. But it was clear from her expression that she had no intention of accepting the decision with grace. She might not make a scene. But she wasn't going to pretend to be happy about it. Richard glowered at his mother, but the look went ignored. He fervently desired his mother's ability to prioritize Susan's desires and joy above her own, if only for a solitary day. But he knew it would be futile to suggest this to her. So, instead, he vowed that he would do everything he could to ensure that Susan had a good birthday, despite their mother's bitter attitude.

Just as their carriage rolled to a stop, the door to Miss Huxley's family's coach opened, and he saw her standing, waiting to disembark. She was stunning in a bright yellow dress with rhinestones and a matching tiara. She noticed him at the same time, and their eyes met. Time seemed to stand still, and Richard was overwhelmed by a maelstrom of feelings. Namely, and competing for his uncertainty, was a growing affection for her. Thomas's suggestion drifted to his mind again, and this time, Richard agreed. They might very well be cultivating something that was more profound than pretense.

Chapter Twenty-one

Anne's heart could have competed with a racing horse as her family's carriage carried Martha and her to Vauxhall Gardens the next day. It was silly, she knew, to be so excited to see a man she was only pretending to court. She tried to tell herself that the true delight came from celebrating Susan's birthday. But when her thoughts kept drifting to Richard, she couldn't lie to herself any longer.

She was so thrilled that she was able to ignore the cool silence inside the carriage. Her parents, though they hadn't admonished her in several days, still rarely spoke to her. Even Charlotte was quiet, content to look out the window as the carriage moved along. Anne was glad that Charlotte was rarely affected by the tension between her older sister and their parents. She just wished that their family didn't have such tensions to begin with. Perhaps, if the duke's and her plan went smoothly enough, the tension would eventually fade. She hoped, at least.

But by the time they reached their destination, the tension was long forgotten. She could see the Thames River, which would carry them to the Gardens, before the carriage had reached it. Along the riverbank, she could see people milling about. She picked out Susan, with her dark curls piled high atop her head and wrapped with a diamond diadem, first among them all. She sat on the edge of her seat, anxious for the coach to stop. Even with her parents there with her, she was looking forward to having another wonderful day.

The gentle breeze off the river caressed Anne as the carriage door swung open. She looked out over the embankment, seeking Susan once more. However, her gaze instantly locked with Lord Richard's. There was something in his eyes that froze her in place. Once again, she felt a connection that suggested more than mere politeness. She knew that if they had been anywhere else, such a prolonged stare might have been considered scandalous. Perhaps, it still would be. But she found that she didn't care.

Susan saw her a second later, running toward the carriage. Anne stepped out quickly, moving aside so her family could disembark and so she could embrace her friend.

"I'm so glad you made it," Susan gushed as Anne wrapped her arms around her friend.

The hug was warm and joyful. And yet, Anne was aware of one more thing. The dowager duchess was staring at her, her cold gaze cutting through the loving moment between friends from the side of Anne's vision. It was all Anne could do to not shudder under the steely gaze.

Charlotte stopped to give Susan a quick hug and Anne a brief kiss on the cheek. Apart from that, Anne's family stepped around her, almost as if she and Susan weren't standing there. Charlotte followed their parents, joining them as they confidently got into the boats along the river's edge. At the same time, Richard approached Susan and Anne, giving her a warm, slow smile.

"Are you ready?" he asked. He turned his chin toward his sister as he spoke. But his eyes never fully left Anne's, making her feel as though he was addressing only her.

"I am," she said, feeling a sudden rush of excitement.

The duke led Susan and Anne to the boat on which the dowager duchess already sat, waiting. Anne swallowed nervously, trying to keep the dowager's demeanor from unnerving her, and failing terribly. Richard helped his sister inside with expert ease, then turned to Anne. He smiled with a hint of mischief in his eyes, extending his hand to assist her. The contact of his warm fingers against her own sent a flurry of sensations coursing through her, quickening her pulse. *What is happening to me?* She marveled as the duke and she took seats beside each other. *One would think he and I are actually courting.*

She tried to shove the thought aside, as she had many times before. But this time, there was no success. Her cheeks continued to grow warm, and she carried on smiling shyly at him as he guided their boat away from the bank. Had he been so handsome at the opera the previous night?

But when the dowager cleared her throat, keeping her gaze indirectly on Anne as she pretended to be interested in the scenery of the river, a horrifying thought occurred to Anne. How could they keep up their ruse with the dowager duchess hovering over them? Could they keep their secret from her, or would she realize they were more friends than courtship partners? And what would she do if the latter should occur?

"Miss Huxley, I must say that I had a wonderful time with you at the opera last night," the duke said suddenly, earning Anne's frantic attention.

She glanced at the dowager duchess, who was pretending to not listen in. Somehow, that was more unsettling to Anne, since she knew that everyone nearby, even in the other boats beside them, could hear their conversation.

"As did I, Your Grace," she said softly.

The duke looked at her, and Anne finally fully met his gaze again. There was warmth and reassurance there, but there was also a sparkle of mischief. He gave her a wink, his lips twitching with a smirk that itched to break onto his face. Then, he straightened his back with a dreamy smile on his face.

"I must confess," he said in a low, conspiratorial voice. "I enjoyed every movement of the opera. And yet, every note paled in comparison to your laughter, Miss Huxley."

Anne's heart skipped a beat, her cheeks flushing with warmth once more. His eyes were magnetic, and she found herself lost in their depths. She searched them for signs of sincerity, or sanity, for saying such a bold thing in front of his clearly disapproving mother. But he merely winked at her again, giving her a small nod indicating that he had meant what he said.

"You are too kind, Your Grace," she said, her joy rising once more, despite the sudden tension in the dowager's body.

The boat ride to Vauxhall seemed to have Susan utterly enthralled. Her eyes danced with delight as she opened her arms wide, gesturing to the entire scene before her.

"Isn't this just wonderful?" she gushed, gazing around dreamily at the water, the other boats, and the glimmer of the lanterns that were just becoming visible on the other bank of the river. "It's positively romantic. It feels like something from a storybook. I could never have imagined how beautiful the river could be."

Anne giggled, looking at her friend with love. She was reminded of why Susan and she were so close. She found joy in the simple things, and she was just as spirited as Anne in many ways. It brought Anne joy to see her friend so happy. But she couldn't help stealing a glance from the corner of her vision at the duke, who was surprisingly looking right at her, rather than at his sister.

"Just wait until we reach the Gardens, Sister," he said, still not looking away from Anne.

Susan squealed softly, earning her a disapproving look from the dowager. The duchess cast Anne a brief, nasty glance, and the message was clear. She believed that Anne was a bad influence on her daughter, never considering that Susan simply had a childlike joy for life, and that she enjoyed expressing it. The glare was cold. But Anne remained resolved to enjoy the evening, if only for the sake of her friend's birthday.

"It's positively enchanting, to be sure," Anne said, giving her friend a warm, bright smile, deliberately ignoring the duchess's attitude. "It's like a special pocket of magic, right here in London."

Susan nodded, and Anne felt sure she had never seen such a smile on her friend's face.

"It is like a dream," she said. "I will cherish this day for the rest of my life."

Anne nodded, allowing herself to take in more of the serene beauty around them. Susan had chosen the word 'romantic' to describe their surroundings and the atmosphere. She had to admit to herself that she agreed with her friend. There was something that inspired every positive feeling that one could experience all at once. And as she cast another glance at the duke, Anne realized that Vauxhall Gardens was a renowned spot for couples. Even though they were there to celebrate Susan's birthday, there was a spark flying between herself and the Duke of Calder that seemingly would not let itself be ignored. It was the definition of elating, and Anne shivered with delight.

But even amidst those moments of bliss, and no matter how hard she tried, Anne couldn't escape the dowager's judgmental glares, which were constantly serving as stinging reminders of the criticisms Anne regularly endured. The thought she'd had before Susan began gushing about how amazing the boat ride and

Vauxhall Gardens was returned. Only this time, it was like a sense of pure foreboding, as if by merely thinking it again, she was breathing life into it and bringing it about. There was every chance that the dowager duchess would find out that Richard and she were only faking their would-be courtship that evening. And the notion was so daunting that Anne could hardly stand to continue contemplating it.

She had shuddered violently before she knew what was happening. She glanced around, hoping no one had noticed. But of course, the duke was looking at her with concern.

"Are you all right?" he asked softly. "Are you getting cold?"

She smiled warmly in response, cursing herself for drawing such attention to herself. If she did not exercise caution, it would be her own conduct that alerted the dowager.

"No, not at all, Your Grace," she said, doing her best to sound sincere. "It was just a momentary chill. It's really quite pleasant out this evening."

The duke smiled at her again, but his eyes still held concern. It was as if, for a moment, he could read her worried thoughts. But eventually, he nodded, looking toward the riverbank, where Vauxhall Gardens was coming into clear view. She held her smile, turning her attention to the scene that was drawing closer to them. But beneath her smile and now forced enthusiasm, her stomach churned with anxiety. What lay at the end of their pretense? Would she still find herself married to her cousin? The idea sent a pang of terror through her, and she had to suppress another shudder. She would rather live the rest of her days as a spinster than to marry Albert. But another, bigger part of her wished that she could, in fact, marry the duke. Had they made a mistake by faking a courtship?

Anne found herself caught in a whirlwind of emotions. She still very much felt the joy of celebrating Susan's birthday. However, the weight of her parents' expectations had returned with her fears about the duchess learning of their ruse, as well as the dowager's palpable disdain for her. And on top of it all, there was the magnetic pull she felt toward the Duke. Everything swirled together within her, creating a storm that felt ready to erupt. She needed to speak to the duke about what was to happen when they were ready to give up their farce. But how long would she have to wait to do that?

Chapter Twenty-two

The sleekly polished wooden boat, which had glided smoothly across the Thames River, finally came to a gentle stop at the dock on the other side. Richard was a bit disappointed that the boat ride was over. He had felt something as he had interacted with Miss Huxley on the ride over. It had been so intense that he couldn't help voicing his secret thoughts about the effect her laugh had on him.

More miraculous was the way she had reacted. She had looked momentarily startled and unsure, as though disbelieving him. He couldn't blame her. They were only supposed to be feigning a courtship, after all. But he had given her his best reassuring look, as well as a scandalous wink. And she had simply smiled sweetly at him, her eyes teeming with joy. Could she be feeling the same thing he was?

The countless lanterns along the dock and riverbank cast a soft, warm glow over the scene, illuminating the lush greenery, while the air reverberated with echoes of faint laughter. The charm of the gardens, which had enthralled his sister, was undeniable. He even admitted, if only to himself, that he agreed with the romantic ambiance present. It was a feeling he was becoming accustomed to of late, and he was coming to enjoy it, as well.

He turned to help the women off the boat, beginning with his mother. The dowager carefully avoided his gaze, but her displeasure was evident in her stiff movements as she stepped away from the boat. Next, he helped Susan, who was looking around at the lanterns and foliage as though under a spell. Miss Huxley was last, and he once again offered her his hand. When their fingers brushed together, as they had when he helped her board the boat, another shiver rushed down his spine. The electric charge between them was palpable, and in that moment, everything else seemed to fade away. The world beyond the two of them ceased to exist, and Richard found himself locked in a gaze that entranced him within its depths. He found himself getting lost there, and he felt that he had never been happier.

What should have been a fleeting moment stretched into the sweetest, most comfortable eternity. Their eyes held one another's as though a safety raft in a high tide. He was aware of nothing but the woman before him, her existence consuming his senses. He stood so close to her that he could almost feel her breath on his skin.

Somewhere in the back of his mind, he had the vague sensation that their lingering eye contact was pushing the boundaries of social decorum. In these conservative times, such an intense connection was dangerous, almost scandalous. But at that moment, he couldn't bring himself to care about propriety or the judgmental eyes of society. Wherever the notion had come from, it wasn't from his conscious. He would stand there, lost in her eyes if he wanted to. And right then, he wanted nothing more.

His mother, naturally, broke the spell between the pair. Her distinct throat-clearing cut through the silence like a shrill crow's caw, shattering the delicate bubble of intimacy that had been forming around Richard and Miss Huxley. Richard blinked as if waking from a dream, and the disapproving glances from his mother were impossible to ignore. She had been watching them closely, her eyes full of rebuke.

Feigning a nonchalant nod to his mother, as though he hadn't been staring at Miss Huxley in a way that society could consider to be unbecoming, Richard led his companion away from the boat and toward the entrance of Vauxhall Gardens. It was as lively a scene as ever, with many clusters of ton members milling about everywhere. Conversations resonated around them, bouncing off the plants and hedges, the sounds of merriment adding to the allure of the place. Richard thought about what Susan had said, about the place having an air of romance about it. He experienced a brief moment of longing, wishing that Miss Huxley was truly his partner, so that they might share in the romantic vibes of the Gardens together.

He couldn't help glancing at Miss Huxley again, noticing how she seemed to be beginning to relax and get the same starry-eyed look that his sister had. He smiled to himself. It was just as important to him that Miss Huxley enjoy herself as it was for Susan to have a good time. And with his mother being so haughty and rigid in her manners, he knew he would have to put all his effort into making the evening lovely for everyone.

The group moved along the promenade at Vauxhall Gardens, their path illuminated by the soft glow of lanterns and the occasional burst of laughter that punctuated the evening air. Miss Huxley's hand rested lightly on his arm, sending wave after wave of tingles down his spine. Each time he touched her, the connection he felt to her intensified. He could no longer give credence to the idea that he was imagining things. There were feelings between him and Miss Huxley. Even if he wasn't sure what they were, or what to do about them.

Their destination, a designated supper box, was still a short walk away, but the world around them seemed to dissolve into a muted blur. Richard found it impossible to focus on anything except for Miss Huxley, especially when she laughed at something Susan had said to her as she grabbed onto her friend's other arm and tugged it like an excited child. On his other side, his mother held her head up high, but the firm set of her jaw told him that her displeasure was only increasing. She had been so obtuse and cold that he noticed when her expression changed. And when it did, it filled Richard with immediate dread. He knew what had changed his mother's mood even before he saw them.

As they approached a junction, the Westbrooks came into view, locking eyes with his mother and himself, respectively. Lady Victoria beckoned for her daughter to join her in a curtsey, which was returned with a flourish by the dowager duchess. Susan and Miss Huxley followed suit reluctantly, but Richard refused to bow. He glowered at his mother, but as always, she failed to notice. He didn't need to guess whether she had arranged such a run-in on purpose. He was sure that that was one of the things his mother had been discussing with Lady Victoria at dinner the evening before.

"What a pleasant surprise," the dowager said, insulting Richard's intelligence as she looked at him pointedly. "It's lovely to see the two of you again."

Richard mumbled something that sounded like a polite greeting, knowing very well that no one would notice his unhappiness. Naturally, Lady Victoria began gushing over his mother's blue dress, while Lady Eleanor looked at him with a smug expression of incredible self-satisfaction, as though she had just won a round of a game that Richard hadn't even known was in play. He supposed she thought she had. Surprising him at his own sister's birthday celebration surely gave her the impression that he was pleased with her efforts to get close to him. But all the encounter had done was deepen his distaste for the young lady and her mother. He intended to do everything he could to ignore the pair. And he would absolutely refuse to allow them to join his family and Miss Huxley for dinner.

"Eleanor, darling, I must say that you look positively radiant tonight," his mother said with a smile. The atmosphere suddenly became heavy and three pairs of eyes turned to Richard as if awaiting confirmation from him. He felt a visceral twinge, recognizing his mother's jabbing slight directed at Miss Huxley. Instinctively, he reached with his free hand and gave Miss Huxley's arm a deliberate squeeze, offering her silent reassurance and a display of solidarity. His desire to protect her flooded him, and he would ensure that he found a way to lessen the sting of his mother's childish, insulting words.

If Mother can do it, I can, as well, he realized, turning to Miss Huxley with the warmest, most charming, and sincerest smile he had ever given her. It wasn't hard to summon the words he sought. They were true, after all.

"You look utterly captivating this evening," he said, leaning in so that only she could hear him, so close that his lips grazed the curl that dangled just over her ear. The delicate rose hue that tinted Miss Huxley's cheeks at his compliment filled Richard's heart with triumph. He had succeeded in erasing the blow that had surely been dealt to her by his mother's words. And now, he got to witness her in all her magnificent beauty as she blushed and smiled shyly at him.

"Thank you," she mouthed silently at him, clearly wanting to continue keeping their little conversation between just the two of them. Richard didn't need to glance back to know that his mother and Lady Eleanor were glaring at him. But when he peeked past Miss Huxley at his sister, he saw the excited, approving expression on her face, barely concealed by the understanding that she needed to temper her reaction. She turned her face away quickly, but not before giving her brother an encouraging wink. It seemed that Susan thought there was more between Miss Huxley and her brother than a farce, as well. And Richard was quickly reaching the conclusion that that was true.

Behind them, Richard heard murmuring, and only then did he remember that the entire Huxley family was in attendance, as well. He glanced back to see Miss Huxley's younger sister covering her mouth with her hand. She had clearly seen the interaction between her sister and him. And the knowing look in her eyes told him that she approved, as well. The viscount and viscountess spoke quietly between themselves, but the viscountess gave him a nervous smile when he made eye contact with her. He recalled the way they spoke to their middle daughter and chastised her for things for which no one should be chastised. He turned back to face the two unwanted women, unsurprised to find that they were both staring at him.

With a sudden rush of resolve, Richard winked at Miss Huxley, inwardly shivering as her blush deepened and her beautiful green eyes glittered with sincere gratitude and delight. Then, he turned back to Lady Victoria and her insufferable daughter, giving them such a small, quick bow that it couldn't be mistaken as anything other than sarcastic and disinterested.

"If you'll excuse us," he said, using all the authority of his station as he spoke. "We really must be getting to our dinner box. I've already made the arrangements for just the seven of us. I do apologise." He made no effort to put any genuine remorse in his final words. Instead, he gave Lady Eleanor the briefest of smug smirks before leading Miss Huxley, followed by Susan and Miss Huxley's family and, reluctantly, the dowager duchess. Beside him, Miss Huxley giggled softly, quickly covering her mouth with her hand. Richard couldn't help smiling at her with deep affection at the sound of her musical laugh.

"Utterly insufferable, those two," he whispered before his mother could catch up to him.

Miss Huxley nodded, smiling up at him sweetly.

"Thank you for being so kind," she said.

Richard shrugged, looking at her earnestly.

159

"I was only being honest," he said.

As their exchanges continued, Richard found himself caught up in emotional turmoil. What had started as a simple charade was evolving into something that was real and undeniable. The lines that delineated reality from make-believe were becoming increasingly indistinct, leaving him contemplating the true nature of their budding relationship. It seemed that Thomas had been right, and that Susan and the younger Miss Huxley knew something he was only just beginning to see. But could he make a real relationship out of what started out as a fake one?

Chapter Twenty-three

The supper box that the Duke had rented was a vision of royal elegance the likes of which Anne had never seen. She had been with her family to Vauxhall Gardens a couple of times, but they had opted for the public dining option once, and the refreshment stalls the second time. The box's chandelier cast a warm, golden glow upon the rich, purple walls.

Anne sat in awe as she looked around, waiting for the duke to order the meal for the evening. It was, unsurprisingly, Susan's favorite meal: roasted duck, salad, freshly baked rolls, and champagne, with syllabubs and strawberry tarts coming for dessert. The savory smells around her made Anne's stomach grumble. For the first time in as long as she could recall, she was excited about dinner.

The seating arrangement was so that her parents and sister sat in a line beside each other, with the dowager and Susan sitting facing them. Anne sat beside across from Susan, and Richard sat beside her at the head of the table. Susan gave her a mischievous wink. Anne blushed and tried to wave her friend away. But the duke noticed and once more gave her a wink of his own, stopping her heart.

"Have you ever been here before, Miss Huxley?" he asked.

Anne nodded, her expression sheepish.

"A couple of times," she said. "But I never got to experience the luxury of a supper box."

The duke grinned at her, raising his champagne glass halfway.

"Well, I do hope you enjoy yourself," he said.

Anne nodded eagerly, beside herself with the wonder of the Gardens.

"It is magnificent," she said.

Susan also lifted her glass, grinning at her friend and her brother.

"This is my favourite place to celebrate my birthday," she said, smiling at the duke. "Thank you for bringing me here, Brother."

Richard finally tore his gaze away from Anne to give his sister a fond, doting smile.

"It's my pleasure," he said, holding his glass upward in a toast. "To the best sister in the world on her special day."

Anne quickly joined the toast with her companions, the gentle clink of the champagne glasses ringing like delicate bells across the table. They drank, and Susan dribbled some of the drink down her chin, causing them all to laugh. As far as Anne was concerned, their respective families, watching them with scrutiny and disapproval, respectively, didn't exist. She was in her own world, and she felt truly happy for the first time in years.

After dinner, the duke led them down the lantern-illuminated path that led to the rotunda, where clusters of nobility gathered around while a small orchestra warmed up their instruments with simple music pieces. The music was intoxicating, mixing with the champagne and the headiness of her confusing, delightful feelings for the duke.

He had left Anne to escort Susan to the dance floor with a man who had asked his blessing to invite her to dance, and people were beginning to stare and whisper. But Anne was in such high spirits that she hardly noticed. It was magical at Vauxhall Gardens, to be sure, and she was enjoying every moment of it. There was so much to experience that she couldn't take it all in quickly enough.

And then, there was the way that the duke had defended her earlier. The dowager duchess's passive aggressive attempt to insult Anne's appearance by gushing over the appearance of Lady Eleanor had hit its mark. But the Duke had noticed right away, despite Anne's lack of outward reaction. He had been quick to help her feel better, and that effort had had its intended effect, as well. For a moment, she had forgotten that her family was trailing behind them as they walked. In that moment, the only thing that had existed was the duke and her. She was vaguely aware that that was occurring more and more frequently lately. It certainly felt to her as though they had a real relationship. And with each touch, secret smile or warm gaze, Anne found herself hoping that such a thing might be possible.

When the duke finally reappeared, Anne's heart swelled with joy. He approached with a warm smile, holding out his hand to her.

"Please, tell me that you'll share this dance with me," he said with the same tone in which he had delivered the heart-stopping compliment just a short time before.

The first notes of the waltz rang through the air, and Anne's heart skipped. She placed her hand into his before she even answered him.

"There's nothing else I'd rather be doing," she said truthfully.

The duke grinned as though she had just handed him a trove of treasure as he led her onto the dance floor. Once again, she forgot everything except for the feel of his hands as he put them into position for the dance, the smell of his sandalwood cologne and the sparkle in his blue eyes as he stared down at her. The longing to kiss him came suddenly and with ferocity, and she had to force herself to breathe as the dance began. From the very first steps, they moved in perfect harmony with one another, both of them seemingly lost in the dance, their gazes fixed firmly on one another. Once more, they were the only people in the world. And Anne relished every second that she remained locked in the dance and lost in his eyes.

Neither of them spoke as the dance carried on, but there was no need for words. The intensity of their bond was apparent in every step. The closeness of his body to hers made her acutely aware of every inch of her skin, and the silent emotions exchanged with mere glances overwhelmed her. Anne was blissfully forced to confront a profound realization, one which came as no surprise, but filled her with a rush of every emotion she had felt all evening. She was deeply, irrevocably in love with the Duke. Her heart ached with the truth of it. Yet, a persistent doubt gnawed at her. Could he possibly share her sentiments? Once again, the doubt about the falseness of their current relationship crept into her mind. Could he really feel something real for the woman he had agreed only to pretend to be interested in?

163

As the final notes of the waltz drifted into the evening air, Anne found herself both exhilarated by the dance and consumed by a whirlwind of emotions. She needed a chance to catch her breath, to have a moment of quiet to herself to work her way through her thoughts and feelings. As the duke smiled at her after escorting her off the dance floor, she gave him a sweet smile, blushing as she noticed he was looking at her as if she was the only woman at the Gardens.

"Thank you for another lovely dance," she said. "I need a little fresh air. Will you excuse me for just a moment?"

The duke smiled, though there was concern in his eyes.

"Of course, Miss Huxley," he said. "Is everything all right?"

Anne nodded, giving him as reassuring of a smile as she could manage.

"Oh, yes," she said. "The dance was just a little exerting. I'll only be a few moments."

Richard nodded in understanding, an understanding that seemed to convey that he knew how she felt. But she tried not to overthink it. She merely curtseyed, turning casually and walking out of the rotunda, trying not to draw attention by running as fast as she could. But the second she was able, she slipped out of view of the rotunda's dazzling lights and hid away in a quiet corner, relishing the cool breeze that caressed her cheeks.

A festoon-adorned hedge beckoned, offering the sanctuary she desperately sought beneath a sky full of stars, while Martha watched over her faithfully. Anne's heart raced, torn between the rush of her newfound love and the uncertainty that clouded her mind. She longed for the courage to reveal her true feelings to the duke. But the fear that he didn't reciprocate was enough to make her second guess herself.

It would be most unseemly for her to express sentiments of affection towards him, given that he is merely excelling in his portrayal as her potential suitor. But could she take that chance? It was clear that Lady Eleanor was interested in him, and that his mother intended to see that match take place. Could she afford to hesitate to confess her true feelings?

Just as she began to lose herself in her musings, a familiar voice pulled her back to reality.

164

"Anne, darling, are you all right?" Susan asked softly.

Anne turned to face her, and the two women shared an unspoken understanding, a silent communion of secrets shared and feelings not yet articulated.

"I've fallen in love with him, Susan," Anne finally said, her eyes finally filling with tears that denoted all the wild emotions she'd been feeling. "I know that was never meant to happen. But it has, and I don't know what I should do."

Susan beamed at her, embracing her tightly.

"It doesn't matter that the two of you started out pretending to court," she said. "Sometimes, love forms under the oddest of circumstance. There's no reason why a relationship that began as a ruse can't develop into something real, something that leads to a happy, shared life where the both of you truly love each other."

Susan's words were meant to offer comfort, and perhaps, they would have. But Anne's focus was suddenly disrupted by a rustling from the hedges. Her heart raced, and she felt a prickling of unease. Had a conversation that was meant to remain private been overheard? The very thought sent a shiver down her spine and intensified her already heightened emotions.

Anne's eyes darted towards the source of the disturbance, which at first was nothing but more of the rustling that had startled her. Susan and she exchanged puzzled glances, and for a moment, Anne thought she had been frightened by a bird or a squirrel. She was just getting ready to laugh at herself when a different noise came from behind the bush that was moving. A moment later, the world fell out from beneath Anne, and she wished that oblivion would swallow her whole.

"Well, well," Sebastian Gray said, his face appearing around the corner with the most sinister of smiles spreading across it. "This is the juiciest gossip yet. I can't wait to tell everyone here. And you can believe that I'm going to do just that."

Anne wanted to move, but she was frozen with fear and shame. She knew Sebastian meant what he said. And the second he told everyone, both the duke and she would be ruined in society. What was she to do?

Chapter Twenty-four: Richard

Richard found it physically painful to pull himself away from Miss Huxley after their dance had ended. So much so that, as soon as he had spoken with his sister to see if she was enjoying her birthday, he set out in search of her. The feelings he had for her were far surpassing those of the nature of their relationship. And he didn't care. The only time anything made any sense to him was when Miss Huxley was by his side.

He was aware of the implications and complexity of his thoughts. After all, at first, the ruse had been merely a way to divert gossip and scandal, to protect Miss Huxley's future, as well as his own. Yet, as the night wore on at Vauxhall Gardens, the magic of the night continued to weave a secret spell on Richard. Every beat of his heart seemed to call out to hers, and with every step he took was a cry from his soul to hear her voice. *What is happening to me?*

It took him a few minutes to clue into the stares and whispers pointed in his direction as he searched for Miss Huxley. He had grown so accustomed to the sneers and rumors that he hardly paid them any heed lately. But something had changed. Now, the whispers grew louder, and the glances cast his way had turned accusatory, laden with judgment. It was as if he had just done some terrible thing for the world to see, and everyone had already labeled him some kind of monster. Every muted conversation he overheard, and every sly smirk his eyes caught deepened his apprehension.

Momentarily distracted, Richard headed toward the center of the rotunda, where the majority of people seemed to be gathered. Something must have happened, and perhaps, if he uncovered what it was, he might find Miss Huxley, or at least figure out where she had gone. But as he made his way through the crowd, his blood froze in his veins, and it was with sheer willpower alone that he was able to keep his feet moving.

"How pathetic you must be to fake a courtship," one woman said to Richard's left. He glanced over to see the woman giving him a look of disgust mixed with smugness.

"And I thought he was such a respectable man," said another woman who Richard vaguely recognized. She was a young lady he had rejected during the previous London Season, and her eyes were ablaze with judgment and distaste. Richard looked away quickly, his heart leaping into his throat. How had this news been discovered? Who could have known? And who could have spread the word in a mere matter of minutes?

Scanning the sea of faces, Richard looked frantically for Miss Huxley. If she were still anywhere nearby, there was no telling what torture she was experiencing. His gaze first caught sight of two women in the distance, and his stomach churned. Their self-satisfied expressions filled Richard with cold certainty that they were the instigators of this chaos. But that still didn't explain how they had heard in the first place. There wasn't a chance that Miss Huxley herself would have told them. Was there?

The puzzle pieces began to fall into place when he spotted Sebastian Gray. Richard wanted to march up to him and demand answers, but the full gravity of the situation settled upon Richard at last. Everyone knew about their little ruse. Everyone including the very people they had sought to avoid marrying. And now, the news had created a scandal the likes of which they could likely never escape. His heart dropped back where it belonged, but it was beating fiercely against his ribs as though it meant to break them. They were caught, and there was no denying it.

Memories flooded Richard's mind of the past few days. He recalled the very moment his sister had mentioned her crazy plan to fake a courtship to him, as well as how quickly he had agreed when he had seen Miss Huxley sobbing her heart out in their parlor the following day. He thought about the feisty determination he had seen in her eyes as she blatantly ignored the whispers each time they were out in public together. He thought about their shared dances, the things he experienced when their hands touched, and the thoughts he had just been having, about how he needed to find her so that he could feel whole again.

And suddenly, as he stood in the midst of the Vauxhall Gardens, under the haughty, disdainful gazes of a society who spent more time shunning people than tending to their own messes, he faced an undeniable truth. He had fallen for Miss Huxley. And not just as part of their charade, but for real, and irreversibly. It was a truth he could no longer deny, one which threatened to consume and liberate him all at once. He was in love with her. And now, the beautiful bond they had created was being destroyed by the toxin that was the opinion of the ton.

Amidst the fresh, disdainful buzzing of the Vauxhall Gardens patrons, Richard was abruptly pulled from his thoughts as he saw Thomas approach. But Thomas's usually jovial face was twisted into a seriousness that was almost eerie on his kind face and filled Richard with abject dread. Even without words, he sensed that Thomas had heard the rampant gossip that now swirled through the rotunda like a cyclone over his pretend courtship with Miss Huxley.

"Are you all right?" Thomas asked, his voice so low that Richard barely heard him with all the noise around them.

Richard gave Thomas a pointed look to convey that he was not.

"Where is she?" he asked, praying that Thomas had seen Miss Huxley.

Thomas shrugged, glancing around briefly before looking back at Richard.

"It seems that everyone knows," he said, raising his eyebrows to convey his unspoken message to Richard.

Richard sighed. He had been sure that was what he'd heard people saying. But some foolish part of him had hoped he had simply misheard or was imagining things because of his own turmoil over the matter.

"I feared as much," he said, pinching the bridge of his nose with his fingertips. "It wasn't received well."

Thomas snorted, but it lacked any humor.

"On the contrary, my friend," he said. "And that's the trouble. Everyone seems rather pleased with such news. These people are true vultures, and they are reveling in light of it all."

Richard appreciated that Thomas never said aloud what it was they were discussing. But it was clear that it no longer mattered. Everyone certainly knew about his secret with Miss Huxley. What he didn't know was what rumors might stem from such new leaking. He also didn't know how Sebastian Gray could have gotten the information in the first place.

"How could he know?" Richard murmured, not meaning to voice the question aloud, but earning a head shake from Thomas, nonetheless.

"I don't suspect that Miss Huxley told him herself," he said. "My guess is that he either bluffed her and she gave him cause to think he was right, or he overheard her talking to someone, like Susan or her maid, about it, and ran with his little morsel of gossip."

As soon as Thomas spoke the words, it all made sense. Of course, Sebastian would have been spying on her. He was constantly trying to make trouble, especially for Miss Huxley. And the malice with which the gentleman had stared at them each time he saw them together spoke of a deep desire to stir problems within the ton for them. Richard gritted his teeth to suppress a low growl. Why couldn't the ton just keep to their own business? Why did they need to dictate and know all about the business of people who weren't doing any harm to anyone?

"What will you do?" Thomas asked, concern in his eyes. "More specifically, what can I do to help you?"

Richard shrugged. He knew he had to tread carefully; he couldn't let the situation get any more out of control than it already had. He wasn't even sure it was possible to reclaim a hold on things now. But he couldn't afford any rash words or actions. And he didn't think that denying the claims would improve the situation. In fact, it might make them appear as if they were guilty of something far worse than fooling ton members. If they didn't already, that was.

As Thomas and he continued to talk, he saw his mother advancing towards them, and the snarl on her face left no question as to what she was thinking. Anticipating a confrontation and unwilling to subject Miss Huxley to such scrutiny, on top of what was already happening, Richard pivoted and began weaving through the crowd, determined to avoid his mother, at least until they were in a less public setting. Truthfully, he didn't think he could face his mother without snapping at her in front of everyone. That would only make matters worse. But right then, he couldn't bring himself to care.

The vibrant sounds of Vauxhall grew faint as he pushed through the people who were now all staring at him. His only concern right then was finding Miss Huxley. However it had happened, he had made up his mind that he would stand with her against the ramifications of the collapse of their ruse. The lantern lights cast flickering shadows on the ground in the shape of the clusters of people who were glaring at him with judgmental eyes, but he ignored them all. All that mattered was Miss Huxley. And when he saw her, his heart sank. She was surrounded by Sebastian, Lady Beatrice and her sneering friends and her own parents, who were scowling at her with the meanest look Richard had ever seen on any parent's face.

The surrounding murmurs became a distant drone as he approached her, no longer caring if he ran into people on his way to get to her. He could hear the scolding her parents were giving her, which ceased immediately as he reached her, glaring at them and using his stature to coax them into stepping back. Their expressions morphed from displeasure to astonishment, but they silently complied with his unspoken demand.

Richard didn't hesitate. He stepped in beside Miss Huxley, a crystal clear display of support and unity with the woman he loved, using his silent, stoic demeanor to offer her a shield against the judgment and whispers of the ton and his presence to give her comfort. She looked so lost and scared, and it broke his heart. He vowed that when that night was over, he would do anything it took to make things up to her. He would do anything to make her his wife. For real this time.

Chapter Twenty-five

All the chatter and tittering laughter fell instantly silent as Richard came to stand beside Anne. She held her breath, her heart pounding fiercely against her ribcage. She quickly looked away, her cheeks flushing with fear and embarrassment. She was sure he was angry with her for letting their secret out to everyone at Vauxhall Gardens that night, and she could hardly blame him. Why had she felt the need to mention it in such a public place, even if she thought Susan and she were alone outside the rotunda?

The silence seemed to stretch on forever, and every single pair of eyes present were fixed solely on the duke and her. Charlotte and Susan were the only ones with sympathetic, concerned expressions on their faces. Everyone else was staring at them with varying degrees of contempt, disbelief, disgust and smugness. Anne thought she might swoon. Part of her hoped she did so that she could escape the silent accusations and judgments of ton members.

Just as she thought she would, indeed, succumb to the discomfort of the situation, Richard reached out and took her hand. She looked up at him timidly to find him smiling at her in a way he never had before. He was not only not angry, but there was more affection in his eyes than in both Charlotte's and Susan's combined. Her heart skipped as she looked into his eyes, waiting for him to speak.

At last, he took a deep breath, his gaze warm and unwavering as his lips parted.

"Anne, there are some things I must tell you," he said. He was addressing her directly, but Anne got the distinct feeling that he intended to have his words heard by all. And he had used her given name in front of a large portion of the ton. What was he planning to say?

"Your Grace, I..." Anne began, intending to apologize to him for the mess she created. But the duke put a gentle finger to her lips, making her heart thump again inside her chest and the tingle she always felt when they touched flood her body, despite the humiliation of the current situation. He gave her a slow smile and one of his trademark winks as he slowly removed his finger from her mouth.

"I am truly sorry for all this chaos, Anne," he said. "But here and now, before the heavens and all these fine people, I wish to clarify some things."

Anne's mouth fell open in astonishment. Why was he apologizing to her? She had realized he meant for everyone present to hear what he had to say. But surely, he couldn't think himself responsible for the proclamation of their false relationship. What had gotten into him.

She tried to speak, but she could find no words. She didn't know what his plan was, and she was afraid of ruining whatever he was trying to do if she continued to speak. So, in the end, she merely nodded, forcing her mouth closed and looking at him with her heartbeat resounding in her ears.

The duke lifted her hand to the level of her bosom, still holding onto it with a gentle grip. But instead of holding it in the prim and proper fashion, he removed first his left glove and then her right one, tucking them into the pocket of his jacket and then lacing his fingers through hers.

"I know there has been a maelstrom of rumours and gossip," he said, his voice carrying through the utterly silent rotunda. "But regardless of what anyone says or thinks, I genuinely care for you, Anne." He paused, giving Lord Gray a cold, pointed look as he spoke again. "While our relationship did begin as mere pretence, which was no one's business but ours," he paused again to turn his gaze back to Anne, his expression instantly transforming into the sweet, affectionate one as before, "I need you to know that the sentiments and the moments we shared have evolved into something profoundly real for me."

Anne's mind reeled, whirling into a frenzy of words and emotions that jumbled together, tripping over one another in her brain and heart and rendering her unable to grasp onto any individual one.

"What?" she asked, feeling a twinge of embarrassment at her lack of meaningful response. Yet Richard simply gave her a doting smile, reaching up with his free hand and gently caressing her cheek.

"Everything I say to you right now is how I truly feel," he said. "I need you to know that, darling."

Anne's heart skipped two beats at the pet name he used. She idly found herself wondering if it was possible for a woman's heart to skip so many times in one evening to send her into a cardiac episode. She blushed, wondering how her thoughts were getting so far away from her. She nodded, silently scolding herself for losing focus.

"I understand, Your Grace," she said.

He gave her one of his classic smirks, chuckling softly. He searched her eyes, looking deeply into them and drawing her into the deepest connection yet. Suddenly, there were no other thoughts, and nothing else in the world mattered, apart from his words, and the brilliant blue of his eyes, which were now gazing at her with a love so powerful it took her breath away. Hope and vulnerability flooded her, and even though her body was paralyzed, she could feel a smile slowly forming on her face.

"I do hope that I can coax you into calling me Richard," he said. "Because I have become utterly smitten with you, my dearest Anne."

Anne's mouth dropped open once more, but the sharp gasp that echoed throughout the room didn't come from her lips. It came from those of her mother, whose mouth was agape just like her middle daughter's. Anne hadn't thought it possible, but after the sudden gasp, the room fell even more silent, as if even the insects had paused their evening songs to listen. The viscount's reaction wasn't as easy to read, though he was watching the conversation take place intently. Charlotte, however, spoke volumes to Anne with her knowing, almost smug smile, and her sparkling eyes.

Everyone else present was also studying the couple. Anne only gave them a brief instant of regard, but she saw that their expressions now ranged from shock and awe to confusion and skepticism. Anne thought a couple of older ladies looked pleasantly surprised with small smiles, but Lord Gray's expression caught her attention just then.

His eyes flickered between disgust and anger, clearly angry that his plan to permanently humiliate the duke and her – Richard and her – in front of the entire ton had failed in such a drastic way. And Anne remained in her own world of shock. Was the man she loved truly telling her that he loved her, as well, in front of a large portion of high society?

"Anne," Richard said softly, bringing her attention back to him once more. "I genuinely mean what I say. I do love you, with all my heart. It was completely unexpected, that much is true. But it is a happy surprise, and I wouldn't change it for anything in the world. I just hope there's a chance that you feel the same way about me."

Anne scoffed with delighted incredulity as a smile crept across her face.

"Richard," whispered, shaking her head in gentle disbelief. "I... yes. I do love you. I am madly in love with you. I just never dreamed that you felt the same. I wanted to tell you before this evening. I was just so afraid that you wouldn't return my affections."

Richard laughed, stepping closer and touching her face again.

"Not only do I return your affections, but I revel in them," he said. This time, as he projected his voice, it seemed as though it was from joy and delight. "And it doesn't matter that you didn't tell me sooner. All that matters is that you've told me now, and I've told you how I feel. Now, there's only one matter left to attend to."

Anne blinked, tilting her head in confusion.

"Oh?" she asked. Her mind was still spinning with the wild events of the evening. She couldn't imagine what he meant. But despite everything he had just said to her, she never could have expected what he did next.

Richard nodded with another wink. Then, he moved to stand beside, rather than in front of, her, still holding her hand gently as he turned to face her parents and sister.

"I do sincerely apologise for having deceived you," he said. "And before esteemed members of the ton, I accept full responsibility for any scandal brought upon your name, should

174

such issues arise. I hope you can forgive me, Lord and Lady Huxley."

Anne watched as her parents exchanged glances. Her mother's mouth was still open, and the viscount gestured to his own chin to urge her to close it. She did at last in the way of trying to say something to Richard, but it seemed as if words had failed her, as well. The viscount, however, looked at Richard with a stunned gaze. Anne had no idea what he was about to say. She just hoped he wouldn't be too hard on Richard.

"I must say this is a highly irregular situation," he said. His words were firm, but his eyes were still filled with confusion. "However, as a gentleman, I feel it is only appropriate to offer forgiveness whenever forgiveness is sought."

Richard grinned, glancing at Anne before continuing.

"Thank you, my lord," he said, bowing. "That means the world to me. But what would mean even more would be if you would grant me your blessing to marry Anne."

It was Anne's turn to gasp, but it was drowned out by the collective gasp of those standing around them. Anne cast a glance at Richard, her gaze widened in astonishment, her bosom aflutter with such intensity that it could have rivalled a spirited stallion galloping across the countryside. She took a deep breath, looking at her sister, who was covering her mouth with both her hands and staring wide-eyed at the two of them.

The viscountess looked as though she might swoon, but she remained silent as she exchanged an uncertain glance with her husband. Clearly, they had been as stunned by Richard's confession as Anne had been. Would they grant their blessing? Or would they be so angry that they sent her away to a convent or disowned her?

The viscount looked at Anne as several emotions flashed across his face. But to her surprise, disappointment was no longer one of them. He studied her for a long moment before looking back to Richard, sighing heavily.

"This is a very strange situation," he said again. "I don't think I would have believed your love for my daughter, had I not heard it for myself. But I have, and I have heard your affections returned by Anne. Thus, I give you my blessing to marry her whenever you wish."

175

Richard's grin grew so wide that Anne thought it would touch his ears. He gave her hand a gentle squeeze as he bowed to the viscount again.

"Thank you very much, Lord Huxley," he said with deep gratitude. "You are a good, honorable, respectable man. I am humbled, both to become part of your family and for the opportunity to love Anne for the rest of our days."

To Anne's surprise, her father bowed in return to Richard, giving him a small but genuine smile. He said nothing, but when he looked at Anne, his smile got a little bigger.

Richard then offered his arm to Anne, looking at her with the love that she had observed in his eyes since he began speaking to her that evening.

"If it would be agreeable to both of you, I would humbly request a private audience with Anne," he expressed. He was addressing her parents once more, but this time, he didn't take his eyes off Anne.

The viscountess spoke then, the spell of the whirlwind of events finally breaking.

"I will consent to this request," she said with a tremble in her voice. "But only if her lady's maid acts as a chaperone."

Richard smiled, bowing to her as he had her husband moments before and nodded.

"Of course, Lady Huxley," he said. "I understand perfectly."

The viscountess nodded, motioning for Martha, who rushed forward through a cluster of people right behind Anne's parents. With her following behind, Richard led Anne to the same place where Susan and she had been talking before Lord Gray tried to ruin their night. However, once they were well out of sight of everyone else, Martha gave Anne a wink and ducked behind a row of hedges, disappearing from view. Anne blushed, silently thanking her lady's maid. Then, she smiled shyly at Richard, who took her hand once again.

"Well, I certainly did not expect such an eventful evening," she said softly. "Did you mean all the things you said? Do you truly love and want to marry me?"

Richard gently pulled her so close that their bodies touched. He cupped her face in his hand and slowly brought his mouth toward hers.

"Does this answer your question?" he asked, his voice husky and filled with an intensity that made Anne's knees weak. Her heart quickened with anticipation, the moment seeming to move in slow motion. Their lips met just as the sky above them burst into a grand display of fireworks. Richard had meant every word. His kiss left no trace of doubt.

Epilogue

The dowager duchess didn't speak a single word to Richard for the rest of their evening at Vauxhall Gardens. He was hardly surprised, although he anticipated a nasty retort when they returned home. Susan, however, threw herself into his arms when Anne and he returned, hand in hand and gazing at each other the way only true love can. The gesture once again captured the attention of the other guests, who were now all speaking in hushed tones in clusters all over the rotunda.

"Brother, I'm so happy for you," she gushed, laughing as she stepped back and wiped tears from her cheeks. "I just knew that Anne and you would truly find love with one another."

Richard smiled, handing his sister his handkerchief and gently rubbing her arm.

"I do hope that all this hasn't ruined your birthday, Sister," he said. "I had no intention of causing such a ruckus or stealing the spotlight from you. But after everyone started being so hateful to Anne, I knew I couldn't allow it to stand. I hope you can forgive me."

Susan looked at him, shaking her head.

"Are you joking?" she asked, her voice rising in pitch as she spoke. "This is the best birthday gift I could have ever received. To know that my brother and my dearest friend are going to have a happy life, and together, to boot, supersedes all my wildest hopes. I just could not be more joyful right now."

Anne giggled beside Richard, earning herself an identical embrace from Richard's sister. Richard grinned at Anne over Susan's shoulder, his heart skipping when he noticed that her cheeks were still flushed from their kiss. That had been the most intense and beautiful moment of his life, and he couldn't wait to share many more of those with Anne.

"So, pray tell, when shall you be united in matrimony?" Susan inquired. "Where shall the nuptials take place? Do you plan on embarking on a wedding journey? Oh, my dear, this is all exceedingly delightful. Whom have you chosen as your bridesmaid and best man?"

Richard laughed heartily, releasing Anne's hand to put his palms on Susan's shoulders.

"You are very excitable, indeed, dear sister," he said with great affection. "I will go first thing tomorrow to procure the license to marry Anne in a month's time. I think that we will be married in the chapel of Calder, since Anne will be becoming the new duchess there. We're not sure if we will be taking a wedding trip. And as far as best man, I have already decided to ask Thomas, if he will accept the task."

Susan glanced between Richard and Anne, puzzled.

"Have you not chosen a bridesmaid yet?" she asked.

Anne and Richard exchanged knowing smiles as Anne took her best friend's hands.

"Susan," she said. "You brought Richard and me together. You granted us the opportunity to fall in love with each other, and I, for one could not be happier. You made all of this possible, and I would be honoured if you would be my bridesmaid."

Susan gasped, covering her mouth with her hands.

"Oh, Anne, darling," she said, embracing her friend again quickly before looking at her with wide eyes. "Would you not rather ask Charlotte?"

Anne shook her head, still smiling.

"I will speak with her," she said. " I am sure she will agree that since you are the reason Richard and I found one another, you deserve the honour. Besides, she's a little young for the role of a bridesmaid. And I think she will be happy to sit and watch the ceremony beside our parents."

Susan clapped, squealing softly with delight.

"Oh, this will be so wonderful," she said. "I gladly accept."

Richard glanced around, noticing that his mother was glaring at him from a hidden corner of the rotunda. Susan followed his gaze, wincing as she saw her mother's expression.

"I think we should probably go home now," she said softly.

Richard looked at her solemnly.

"Are you sure, Sister?" he asked.

Susan beamed at her brother and nodded.

179

"I'm positive," she said. "I have had the loveliest birthday ever. But tomorrow, I want to awaken early and be fresh and full of energy. The wedding is in one month, and we have so much planning to do."

Anne and Richard both laughed. It touched him to see how thrilled his sister was. And he was glad that their debacle hadn't ruined her birthday, after all. He offered his sister one arm and Anne the other, smiling fondly at them both.

"Then let us depart," he said, flashing his mother a wide smile as he nodded meaningfully at her and guided the two women back towards the boats.

Susan was a bundle of energy and chatter on the boat ride back to the other side of the river, practically skipping as Richard bade Anne and her family a good night and then led her and his mother to their carriage. He couldn't get a word in on the trip home, and Richard didn't mind at all. His mind was still reeling, and he was happy to let his sister gush about her ideas for bridal bouquets and the bridesmaid's dress that Anne and she would pick out together. The dowager duchess was expectedly silent, staring out the window. But for the first time, her broody pouting didn't faze him at all. He was genuinely happy and in love, and not even his mother could ruin that for him.

When they returned to Calder Manor, however, his mother grabbed his arm as soon as Susan skipped off to her chambers. She pulled him toward her, her eyes flaming and her nostrils flaring.

"This is unacceptable," she hissed. "I will not let this stand."

Richard pulled out of his mother's grasp by firmly yanking away his arm.

"You will," he said. "I love Anne. I am to marry her in one month. And you will not stop me."

Her mouth fell open, her expression morphing into one of indignation.

"I am your mother, Richard," she said. "I know what's best for you. You cannot marry a woman like Anne Huxley. We have discussed her reputation, and how I feel about her. I will not be so easily dismissed."

Richard looked down at his mother, surprising them both by giving her a tender smile.

180

"After this evening, I think she and I will both have quite a reputation, wouldn't you agree?" he asked.

The dowager duchess huffed.

"That's another thing," she said, sounding defeated even as she continued arguing. "I cannot believe you would fake a courtship with a woman while Lady Eleanor was so eagerly trying to win your affections."

Richard shrugged.

"I could never have loved her, Mother," he said. "Anne is my one true love. I am going to marry her. I only hope that one day, you come to accept this."

The duchess put her hands on her hips, staring at Richard with tired disbelief.

"I will never accept her," she said. "I hope you will reconsider."

Richard shook his head as he turned away from his mother.

"I will not," he said. "My decision stands. I am in love with Anne, and she will be my wife."

With that, he walked calmly to his chambers. Even the argument with his mother had done nothing to dampen his high spirits. He would marry Anne, indeed. And their wedding day could not come soon enough.

***

The following month passed in a blur. Susan practically lived with Anne while they planned the wedding. The dowager duchess stayed locked in her chambers, refusing to see him or entertain any company. Even though the gossip and scandal dissipated inside that month in favor of fresher, juicier tales, the dowager turned a blind eye and stood her ground on her proclamation of rejecting Anne. And when she still hadn't said anything to him the night before his wedding, he began to wonder if his mother might never, in fact, accept Anne as her daughter-in-law.

The wedding day was chaotic. Watson prepared Richard's bath, which Richard enjoyed while the valet ensured that his dark green brocade suit was spotless and free of creases and wrinkles. After his bath, Watson dressed him with great care and combed back his hair.

Despite its elegance, it was a style more typical of regular social events, as was the color of his wedding suit. But he was marrying a free-spirited woman, one whose personality and fun-loving nature was refreshing and inspiring to him. He could hardly wait to spend the rest of his life pushing the norms of society with her. Starting with their wedding day.

Just as Watson was about to finish, there was a soft knock on his door. Expecting Susan in her pale pink satin bridesmaid's dress, he hurried over and opened the door with a wide smile on his face. But his smile melted into puzzlement when he saw his mother standing there. She looked him over with an unreadable expression. Then, she entered the room when he stepped aside to invite her in. She spoke before he could.

"Richard," she said, seemingly measuring her words with care. "I have been against this wedding from the very beginning. I'm still not certain that I approve, to be honest."

Richard sighed. He hadn't expected her to accept the decision, or even attend the wedding. But was she really going to try to talk him out of it again on the day?

"Mother, it's almost time," he said. "I do not wish to fight with you right before my own wedding."

But the dowager duchess shook her head slowly, looking at Richard in the same way she had in the doorway. Only this time, he recognized the expression, as foreign as it was on his mother's face. It was sheepish and repentant, and his words stopped in his throat.

"I'm not here to fight," she said. "During the past month, I have witnessed more joy and happiness in you than I've seen since you were a boy. I tried to deny it, which is why I avoided you except at meals. But I've overheard you talking with Susan, and I see the way your face lights up at any mention of Miss Huxley's name. While I still have some reservations, I know now that I need to give her a chance. I support your marriage to her, and I will accept her as my daughter-in-law."

Richard grinned, pulling his mother into a warm embrace.

"That means everything to me, Mother," he said. "Thank you."

The dowager duchess pulled away from her son and wiped a tear from her cheek.

"It's almost time," she said. "May I escort my son to our carriage one last time before there is another woman to do it for me?"

Richard's heart squeezed at the sudden show of sentiment, and he nodded.

"I would be delighted, Mother," he said.

Richard, flanked by his mother and sister, boarded the carriage, his heart lighter and happier than ever before. He hadn't thought it was possible to be full of more joy than he was with the knowledge that he was on his way to marry the woman he loved more than anything in the world. But as he listened to his mother and sister talk about how different things would be with a new duchess, his heart felt filled to bursting. His mother's willingness to accept Anne had stunned him. But he had never been more grateful to, or proud of, his mother in his entire life. It seemed like all the important women in his life would get along, and that was something more valuable than all the gold in England.

The ceremony was a blur for Richard up until it was time for the couple to exchange their vows. Then, time stood still as he stared into Anne's jade green eyes and professed his eternal love for her, and heard hers for him professed, in front of their closest friends and family. Even as the words were exchanged, he could hardly believe he was marrying his sweet, beloved Anne, who looked like a vision in her pale orange silk wedding dress that had a small, almost imperceptible pair of cat eyes embroidered on the left shoulder of the dress.

He suppressed a laugh when he noticed it, but he found a way to subtly stroke the eyes with his fingertip when he pushed back her pale orange veil and gave her a wink. She grinned, knowing that he noticed it and they shared a secret look, even as their loved ones applauded the proclamation that Anne was now the new duchess of Calder. And when they kissed, Richard's heart pounded fiercely in his chest. She was now his bride, and he was completely enraptured.

There was one more thing he noticed. As they stood beside their respective friends, Susan and Thomas were exchanging meaningful, clandestine looks with one another. Richard realized immediately that there was an emerging bond forming between them. He had always thought he would shudder when the day came that his sister would find herself a serious suitor. But as he met Thomas's eyes and noticed the flush of a man who was utterly smitten with a young lady, he couldn't help but smile. He knew that Thomas was a good, honorable man, and if he captured his sister's heart, that was all right with him.

After they signed the wedding registry, Richard escorted his new bride back down the aisle of the little Calder chapel. They were congratulated with tears and smiles, and plenty of pats and embraces. And from there, the newlyweds and all their guests moved onto the Huxley estate, where Lady Huxley had prepared a sumptuous wedding breakfast. As straggling guests continued to arrive, the viscount pulled Richard aside and offered his hand.

"Congratulations, Your Grace," he said. "We are thrilled to have you join our family."

Richard took the handshake eagerly, smiling brightly at his new father-in-law.

"The honour is mine, to be sure," he said sincerely. "Thank you both for this breakfast. For everything."

The viscount bowed stiffly before nodding and offering Richard a small smile.

"It's our pleasure, Your Grace," he said.

The viscountess approached the couple, gently guiding them toward a long table which had been set up along the back edge of their ballroom dance floor.

"I've arranged it so that you can receive your gifts first, then we shall begin the dancing," she said.

Richard looked at Anne, who was beaming happily at her mother.

"Thank you so much for all of this, Mother," she gushed.

The viscount gave her a contrite look, folding her hands together.

"It's the least we could do, darling," she said. Though she didn't elaborate, Richard understood what she was saying. Like his own mother, Anne's parents regretted their initial behaviors and reactions. They were all trying to make amends in their own ways. And Richard knew that Anne was as pleased as he was.

One by one, the guests lined up with their respective gifts and words of congratulations. As each guest walked away Anne and Richard put their gifts on the long table, preparing to receive the next ones. When it was the dowager duchess's turn, she approached with a small silver box that Richard recognized, and his heart leapt into his throat.

"Welcome to our family, Anne," she said, holding out the box. "These belonged to my mother. Now, I'd like for you to have them."

Richard watched, shocked, as Anne uncovered his grandmother's heirloom diamond earrings. She gasped softly, touching them reverently and smiling up at the dowager duchess with tears in her eyes.

"This is such an honour," she said. "Thank you, Your Grace."

The dowager shook her head, awkwardly patting Anne's arm.

"Since you are now my daughter-in-law, please, call me Adelaide," she said.

Anne embraced her, catching the dowager off guard. But Richard's heart swelled with renewed pride when his mother hugged Anne back.

"Thank you for everything, Adelaide," Anne said softly.

Just then, there was a thud behind the little group. They all turned to find one of the packages on the floor and an orange bundle of fur sitting where it had once been. Mischief seemed to sense the eyes on him, as he turned to glance over his shoulder. He gave Richard a slow blink, stepping over the other packages to demand pets from him and Anne, who immediately complied. Much to his surprise, the dowager duchess chuckled, which became contagious throughout their guests and the party hosts. It seemed that everyone was warming to Mischief's antics, and Richard smiled fondly at the feline.

"Good boy," he murmured, planting a kiss on the top of his head.

The cat began to purr, rubbing against Richard's face on his way to get a kiss from Anne. And everyone cooed.

The celebrations continued all throughout the day, reaching their zenith as Anne and Richard found themselves alone on the terrace late that afternoon. Anne turned to him, her eyes filled with love, and Richard, unable to resist, drew her into his arms.

"I can hardly believe this is real," she whispered, despite it only being the two of them on the terrace. "I dreamed of being your wife. And now, I am."

Richard nodded, cupping the back of her neck gently in both his hands as he leaned closer to her.

"You are," he said. "You are my wife, my duchess, and the most wonderful woman I have ever known." He paused, giving her a sweet, lingering kiss, shivering as the electricity, more intense than ever before, coursed through his body. "I love you, my darling Anne."

Anne smiled up at him, kissing him again and again.

"And I love you," she said.

Extended Epilogue

"Richard, darling," Anne said as she rapped on the door of her husband's chambers. "Are you ready? We must leave shortly to make it to the church."

There was silence behind the door, lasting long enough for Anne to knock again. She was about to call to Richard again when the door creaked open. She glanced down, realizing that it hadn't been latched all the way, so her knocking pushed it all the way open. She stepped inside the room, hearing soft, muffled laughter coming from near the bed, on top of which she now noticed that Edward, Anne's and Richard's two-month-old son lay. Frowning, she approached the bed, jumping back in surprise as an orange blur moved into her line of vision, landing on the bed between her and the infant.

"Mischief," she said with a laugh as she reached out to stroke the feline. He allowed her fingers to graze him only briefly before turning up his tail at her and promptly curling up protectively at Edward's side. The baby was swaddled comfortably in a clean blanket, and he was awake but seemingly content to look at the ceiling with eyes that were only just learning how to focus. But where was Richard?

Another louder chuckle came from the other side of the bed. Anne laughed again when she realized where Richard was. Sure enough, as she peered over the edge of the bed, she saw him crouching on the floor with Mischief's ball of yarn, preparing to attempt to entice the feline to play with it. Anne reached to adjust the blanket to rest further up on her young son's chest. But Mischief reached out and slapped her hand away, his paw hovering in anticipation of another attempt to touch her child.

"What's this?" she asked, reaching to pet the cat again. Once more, he pushed her hand away, then gently rested his head across the infant's stomach. Anne scoffed, though there was no real offense or indignation in the sound. At this, Richard peeked over the bed, his laugh not muffled by his proximity to the bed and floor that time.

"My apologies, darling," he said, shaking his head as he pulled himself off the floor. "But it seems that, since little Edward entered our lives, Mischief has forgotten your existence entirely."

Anne gave her husband a playful nudge with her fingertips, shaking her head and laughing at the joke that had become common with them since Edward's birth. It was true enough. Ever since the arrival of the baby, Mischief had begun to become more and more attached to him.

"And you thought you could make him notice you more?" he asked.

Richard shrugged, not looking at all embarrassed of having been caught trying to play on the floor with the feline just minutes before needing to leave for his son's christening.

"I thought I could try," he said. "What's the worst that could happen?"

Anne glared playfully at her husband, reaching out her hand toward the cat. As she expected, Mischief promptly swatted at it, and she gave Richard a pointed look.

"See?" she asked.

Richard laughed again, reaching out to pet the animal. None to her surprise, Mischief let Richard scratch him behind the ears, and she rolled her eyes jovially at her husband.

"Come, darling," she said. "We'll be late if we don't hurry."

Richard chuckled once more, reaching over to the chair beside his dresser and fetching the dark blue jacket that matched the breeches he was clad in.

"I'm ready, my love," he said, smoothing out the creases in his breeches and putting on his jacket. "And Edward is already wearing his christening gown."

Anne smiled fondly at her husband. He was just as free-spirited as her, which was one reason she adored him so. But he was also responsible, which was another thing she loved.

"Very good," she said, walking over to give him a quick kiss as she swooped in and picked up the child despite Mischief's slaps and mewls of protest. "Then we should be just on time."

Richard grinned, putting a gentle arm behind her back and leading her out of the room.

"Are you surprised?" he asked.

188

Anne laughed again.

"I found you playing on the floor with a cat's toy, didn't I?" she retorted.

The couple shared a laugh as they headed out to the carriage as a family. And as they boarded the coach, Anne realized that she wouldn't have rather found Richard any other way.

Richard had taken care of all the arrangements to see that a grand affair was organized to celebrate their son's christening. By the time they arrived at the church, Anne saw that all their family and close friends had gathered, filling the sanctuary of the church where they were married with warmth and love once more.

The viscount was the first to approach, followed closely by both Anne's and Richard's mothers.

"Hello, my dear Anne," he said softly, gazing lovingly down at the wrapped bundle in her arms. "May I hold him?"

Anne giggled.

"It seems that everyone prefers Lord Edward to me," she said with the wink she had picked up from Richard.

Everyone laughed merrily, but they were quickly enthralled by Edward as he reflexively raised his tiny fist and began making soft sounds with his mouth. Richard put an arm around Anne's waist as their loved ones took turns holding their baby boy, smiling down at her.

"Now I see how you feel," he said, glancing toward the dowager duchess, who was cooing softly to the infant.

Anne giggled again, resting her head on his chest.

"I still love you, sweetheart," she said.

Richard grinned.

"Likewise, my love," he said.

The ceremony commenced a few minutes later, led by the round, friendly vicar of Calder. He opened with a prayer, followed by a speech about the importance of baptism for those as innocent as young children and reading a passage out of the bible on the same subject. He said another prayer for safety, luck and prosperity for little Edward. Then, he looked at all the guests with a warm smile.

"Will the people chosen as godparents please step forward?" the vicar asked.

189

Hand in hand, Thomas and Susan, happily married for six months, stepped toward them with glowing smiles on their faces. They recited their duties and promises for little Edward in their roles as his godparents, assuring their loved ones and God that they would have his best interest at heart, always. Shortly after, the ceremony concluded, at which point the dowager duchess couldn't approach fast enough to scoop up her grandson from the vicar.

Thomas cleared his throat, raising his hand in the air.

"Before we leave the church, could we have a moment of your attention?" he asked. "This place has seen so many of our loved ones' special moments, and we'd like to share something special with you all now."

Everyone murmured their consent, looking at the couple expectantly. Even the vicar, who had been writing down things for the church records regarding the baptism, gave Thomas and Susan an encouraging nod.

Thomas put an arm around his new wife, and with broad smiles they spoke in unison.

"We're expecting our first child," they said, looking at each other in shock at the synchronization of their announcement before laughing giddily.

The dowager duchess gasped loudly, rushing over to embrace her daughter.

"Oh, darling," she said, holding Susan tightly. "Congratulations, my sweet daughter. I am so happy for the both of you."

Richard chuckled softly, leaving Anne's side and walking over to his mother and sister. He reached out and gently took Edward from her, giving both women a kiss on their cheeks.

"Hey there, Mother," he said, winking at her. "In your mirth, you almost crushed your grandson."

The dowager gave her son a playful push with the palm of her hand, but she was smiling brightly and there were joyful tears in her eyes.

"Oh, nonsense, dear," she said, but she allowed her son to take his son back over to Anne. She took the baby, admiring how precious he looked in his christening gown.

Richard then turned back to face his sister and her husband again, offering Thomas a hearty handshake.

"Truly, congratulations to the both of you," he said. "This is joyous news and I know we can hardly wait to have another addition to our family."

Thomas naturally accepted the handshake, pulling Richard into a warm hug.

"Thank you, my good man," he said. "Fatherhood just looked so good on you that I needed to try it for myself."

Richard glanced back where Anne stood, gently rocking the infant, who was now drifting off to sleep in his mother's arms after all the excitement of his baptism.

"It's the best thing I've ever done, next to being a husband," he said.

Anne grinned at her husband, as did Thomas.

"If fatherhood is anything like husband-hood, I have no doubt that I will be in heaven," he said.

Richard nodded, not taking his eyes off Anne.

"You certainly will," he said softly.

Charlotte rushed up to where Anne was standing, nearly knocking her over.

"Anne, you won't believe it," she said. She was clearly very excited and out of breath.

Anne laughed merrily, patting her sister gently on the back.

"Take a breath, Sister," she said. "What won't I believe?"

Charlotte's green eyes were sparkling, and she looked ready to burst. Anne held her breath, wondering if she was about to announce a courtship of her own.

"I can't believe you haven't heard," she said, still gasping. "Mother told me that Albert was recently married to a young baron's daughter. Apparently, he's found true love with her."

Anne blinked, surprised. She hadn't thought about him since Richard and she began their ruse. Now that she thought of it, however, she realized she couldn't recall her parents saying anything about his feelings regarding losing his chance to marry her.

"Well, that explains quite a bit," she said, musing aloud.

Charlotte nodded, clapping her hands together.

191

"And that's not all," she said. "Elizabeth told me that Lord Gray has married Lady Eleanor."

At the mention of Lady Eleanor's name, Richard looked up and blanched, moving closer to Anne and putting an arm around her waist.

"What about her?" he asked.

Anne giggled, patting his chest gently.

"Do not fret, my love," she said. "She isn't still pursuing you. Charlotte just told me that she married Lord Gray."

Richard's face instantly brightened as he grinned.

"Well, how about that?" he said with a chuckle. "I'm sure they'll be quite happy together."

Anne made a face, but her heart was too full of joy to be bitter.

"They should have plenty of time for their gossip now," she said.

Everyone laughed.

The End

Printed in Great Britain
by Amazon